Andrew Leigh

Conversations
with
Marvellous
MUSES

WWW.ANDREWSBOOKS.SITE

CONTENTS

OPENER

This is a journey to meet Marvellous Muses. Sometimes, they are people famous in their own right. Others remain invisible or lost in the shadows. Let's meet one muse who refuses to stay in the background.

It's May 29, 1913, and the Théâtre des Champs-Élysées in Paris is full to bursting. Dread and thrill hang in the air. The opening night of The Rite of Spring is the new production from the Ballets Russes, and the audience is buzzing with anticipation. Many want a moment of artistic breakthrough; others are ready for scandal.

The curtain is about to go up on what will be remembered as one of the most notorious nights in cultural history. The orchestra tunes up noisily under Pierre Monteux's baton. With its jarring rhythms and discordant harmonies, Stravinsky's groundbreaking score awaits its first public hearing. Backstage, the great dancer of his time, Nijinsky, gets ready to guide his dancers through choreography so bold, so elemental, so primitive, it'll appal even the most avant-garde reviewers.

Overseeing it all in the wings is Sergei Diaghilev, a real-life muse without whom it was all impossible. Diaghilev, to some, is a genius who has transformed ballet into 21st-century art and has put Russian art at the leading edge of European culture. To others, he is a provocateur whose audacity and ambition strike at the heart of tradition itself. Tonight, it is he who plays both parts.

Diaghilev watches intently. His eyes scan the stage as the lights dim and silence falls over the audience. He is the unseen force behind every element of the production - the one who discovered Nijinsky's extraordinary talent, inspiring him to produce genuinely innovative choreography. He commissioned Stravinsky's audacious music and nurtured Roerich's avant-garde designs. As a muse, he is the weaver of this entire tapestry of rebellion and creativity.

The performance begins, and the audience is immediately divided. Gasps turn to murmurs, then outright shouting as Stravinsky's music crashes through the theatre and Nijinsky's angular, otherworldly choreography unfolds. People stand, some in protest, others in awe. The crowd's noise competes with the orchestra, but Diaghilev remains still, his expression unreadable.

He lives for this moment, for the energy of creation and the chaos it breeds. Diaghilev is a patron of the arts and a muse in the finest sense. He doesn't just inspire; he mines the potential in his collaborators to create and expand beyond the limits of what they think they are capable of. He has influenced the work of many, not as a passive presence in the background but through his demands for nothing less than brilliance.

On this night, Diaghilev's vision alters the trajectory of art. He has played a key role on stage and across music, dance, and design, reinventing modernism for today. This night is glorious; to others, it is notorious. But no one who was there could deny that they had witnessed the power of a muse in action.

As the curtain falls to a storm of applause and outrage, Diaghilev stands silent in the wings. The chaos on stage reflects the daring fire that burns within him. His muse mission for the moment is complete.

WHAT IS A MUSE?

The idea of the Muse has shifted dramatically - from divine whisperers to creative collaborators, from passive idealists to fierce co-creators.

In Greek mythology, the Muses were divine sisters who presided over the arts and sciences. The Muse Calliope inspired people to create epic poetry and to express themselves eloquently. Melpomene inspired people to be creative about tragedy, while the Greek Muse Thalia encouraged them to make comedy and pastoral poetry.

All nine Muses were daughters of Zeus, king of the gods and Mnemosyne, the goddess of memory. They were usually described as graceful and artistic figures who lived in places of creative inspiration, such as Mount Parnassus.

Later, the Romantics were a group of artists, poets, writers, and thinkers from the late 18th to the mid-19th century who emphasised the idea of the artist's inner Muse - a deep, personal wellspring of creative energy.

They saw inspiration as something almost mystical and organic, rather than as a gift from an outside deity. Nature itself was a Muse for them. William Wordsworth regarded nature as a living force that could unveil profound truths to the receptive spirit.

However, even in such depictions, the Muse was seldom passive. They were someone to bounce ideas off of, to challenge you intellectually, emotionally, and creatively.

The Romantics often used the actual women around them as Muses, even as they idealised and sometimes stifled their possibilities.

Percy Bysshe Shelley referred to Mary Shelley as his Muse, while Dante Gabriel Rossetti, a later Romantic-influenced Pre-Raphaelite, famously modelled and idealised Jane Morris as his Muse.

However, women like George Sand and Virginia Woolf resisted the idea of a passive Muse and became creators instead.

For the Greeks and later the Romantics, "Muse" meant a woman. Even today, "Muse" often conjures an image of a woman being gazed upon, rather than a force gazing back.

It often implies women inspiring male artists. Yet, as my conversation with musician Prince and the earlier mention of Diaghilev show, a muse can be anyone, regardless of sex or gender, who stokes the fires of creation.

Or imagine T. S. Eliot drawing inspiration from Ezra Pound, or Maya Angelou finding her voice because of the survival of those who came before her.

The Muse no longer represents an objectified figure, a static entity upon whom the creative genius bestows the gift of creativity. Instead, it means an active force that challenges and transforms the world in which they exist.

Sometimes, a Muse becomes necessary for the continued existence of its focus of attention. Gala Dalí is a Muse who doubles as a hard-nosed critic, protector, and agent. When she died, her husband, the artist Salvador Dalí, had no more reason to live and faded away.

The idea of a Muse can also transcend individuals. That is, the Muse becomes symbolic, representing a theme, a concept, or an internal drive. A universal idea, such as freedom or Dr. Schweitzer's famous philosophy of Reverence for Life, can inspire people far beyond any actual personal contact.

THE CONTEXT

Many of the Muses I spoke with lived in the 19th and early 20th centuries, a time of profound societal and cultural transformation.

In some places and countries, a flourishing salon culture of intellectuals gathering in people's homes existed. This social gathering offered spaces where ideas and artistry could transcend gender and class barriers.

Yet even in these progressive environments, the contributions of Muses were often overshadowed by the creators they inspired.

Pauline Viardot, a celebrated French mezzo-soprano born in 1821, was renowned for her theatrical and operatic roles, as well as her compositions.

Yet she also had an intense, muse-like relationship with Ivan Turgenev, the more renowned Russian novelist who popularised Russian literature in the West. Viardot inspired novels, librettos, and musical compositions.

Another real-life Muse, Lou Von Salome, famously inspired many others. Due to her translations of his esoteric writing, Nietzsche exploded onto the international scene. Meanwhile, Sigmund Freud anxiously waited for her to be present in the audience before launching into one of his popular lectures.

Von Salome also helped the renowned poet Rilke rise above pedestrian poems to something more divine. Despite her powerful impact, Von Salome was often overshadowed by those she inspired.

With the aid of their Muse, other gifted souls charted a course around society's restrictions, leaving durable marks on the cultural landscapes of their eras.

Marvellous Muses reveals just some of these lives, putting them front and centre, rather than being a supporting character in someone else's story.

HOW REAL ARE THE CONVERSATIONS?

How reliable are these fictitious conversations? All are based on careful research, high-quality biographies, published letters, Britannica summaries, and numerous online sources.

Ultimately, they are products of my imagination, not just formal historical evidence. Judith Zineer, in her well-rounded biography of the early physicist Émilie du Châtelet, explains how fully fledged biographers must cope with profound contradictions about their chosen subject. She spells out the dilemmas of interpreting so-called evidence.

Even the finest biographers must often infer what their subject meant or said based on their various comments or actions. These twenty conversations with Marvellous Muses rely on biographical sources, but as one expert points out:

"All biographies are a collection of holes tied together with string" - these imagined dialogues thread those gaps with wonder, respect, and a little risk.

If you wish to learn more about the twenty chosen Muses, I have provided some limited biographical references at the end of each conversation that you may find helpful.

MY PURPOSE

The device of a conversation enabled me to imagine hearing directly from these Muses and what they might say about their lives. While the Muses were chosen using carefully devised criteria, ultimately, their final selection relied on personal preference.

These are the voices I longed to hear and the questions I most wanted to ask. I hope you find their company as arresting, enriching, and unexpected as I did.

ÉMILIE DU CHÂTELET

1706–1749

Émilie du Châtelet was a Muse and an influential intellectual figure in 18th-century France. Her physics, mathematics, and philosophy work earned her an enviable reputation. Émilie contributed to understanding Newtonian mechanics and was almost certainly one of the first women physicists.

Beyond her scientific achievements, Émilie's influence extended to inspiring many great thinkers, particularly Voltaire. Her role in shaping the intellectual climate of the Enlightenment was significant, as she overcame the challenges of being a woman in a male-dominated field. She made an enduring impact on science and culture.

ÉMILIE DU CHÂTELET

It is the morning in 1737, and Émilie du Châtelet sits under the shade of an ancient oak tree in the gardens of her beautiful Château de Cirey in France. It's sunny and there is a strong scent of flowers.

She is studying some text and clearly waiting for my arrival. As I approach, she sets aside her small book and gestures for me to sit beside her.

"Ah, how pleasant it is to speak without the constraints of a formal setting! I often prefer the solitude of nature, away from the crowds, where the mind can breathe and expand. Tell me, what has brought you to Cirey? Surely not just the beauty of the landscape?"

Indeed, Madame du Châtelet, I've come to learn more about you, your life, and your work. Most of all, given your involvement with that great thinker Voltaire, I want to explore your role as a Muse.

"Certainly, when I'm not engaged in domestic responsibilities and supervising the care of my children, Françoise-Gabrielle-Pauline, Louis-Marie-Florent, and Victor-Esprit, I conduct experiments on the nature of energy and motion. I confess I am eager to discuss these ideas with you."

Madam, your involvement in science is well known. There's a story that you were immensely curious as a child and discovered how to use a pair of dividers at age three.

"Oh, poof! I can scarcely remember being that young, let alone playing with instruments. I hope the rest of our conversation will be on more solid ground!

Still, I was a curious child, and my mother encouraged me to be so. But she was too busy to devote time to me, running a household equivalent to a large hotel."

And your father?

"The king much-favoured him, so he hardly had any spare time. Even when he did, he would spend it with my brothers.

Still, I was lucky to be born into an aristocratic family in 1706 and given a rare education for a woman. It's true I grew up loving instruments that measured, drew shapes and weighed things.

Like some of my contemporaries, I didn't go to school. Though I still have a talented tutor, my studies are now mainly self-directed and provide an essential foundation for my intellectual development.

My father hoped I would be content to marry. Well, I did at nineteen, but my poor father did not anticipate that I would still devote myself to philosophy, mathematics, and the natural sciences.

My tutors introduced me to the great works of our time, but my innermost passion guided my path.

I have struggled against many of society's norms, and my desire to understand the universe's workings has always been my driving force."

Yes, it seems that nothing can hold you back.

"There are moments, of course, when my gender has been a barrier. Men often underestimate me, thinking my mind is occupied with more trivial pursuits.

But as you say, Monsieur, I have never let that hold me back. I do not demand recognition because I am a woman, but because my work deserves to be heard.

I find myself challenging not only the ideas of the past but also the very structure that limits women's intellectual contributions. In time, women like myself will hopefully not be seen as exceptions but as equal participants in the grand experiment of human knowledge."

What, then, Madam, are your thoughts on metaphysics and the nature of knowledge? How have they influenced your scientific work?

"I view science and philosophy as intertwined. Some scientific colleagues see them as separate realms. While I respect their opinions, I see things differently. To me, understanding nature means asking how and why it works in such a way.

Newton's laws attract me because they are not mere mathematical formulas. Instead, they provide a deeper understanding of the world and disclose a sublime harmony between reason and nature.

I have no illusions that my theories will be accepted immediately. I know that time will be my judge.

However, I am proud to know my ideas are being passed along, expanded upon, and refined. In the future, perhaps my thoughts on energy and light will spark great discoveries in physics."

That tells me so much about how you think and act. Can you perhaps also say something about those with whom you are working?

"Jean le Rond d'Alembert is my tutor and mathematical adviser. Our conversations have been invaluable to me. His mathematical brilliance joins my philosophical musings as we explore science's vast territories.

Here at Cirey, I enjoy a rich intellectual exchange with many visiting thinkers eager to share ideas and discuss the great questions of existence, knowledge, and nature. This estate has become a small learning centre, a refuge for the mind. She laughs softly: "Many, though, do not realise that I am another passionate soul, hungry for knowledge and the thrill of discovery."

They once told me a woman's brain would overheat if she studied too hard. I told them if that were true, I'd have burned down all of Cirey by now."

You are too modest, madam. Your thoughts and ideas are as sharp as any man's. Your contributions to science, particularly your work on the nature of light and energy, are groundbreaking. How did you first come to study these fields?"

"Light and energy. Two of the most fascinating mysteries of nature. My path towards this phenomenon began most unexpectedly.

Women in my class are mainly encouraged to pursue accomplishments of more traditional types - beauty, social graces, and music. But I always had a curious mind that didn't fit neatly into the receptacles people tried to put me in.

In the salons of Paris, I encountered men of great intellect, some of whom became my closest collaborators. For instance, Voltaire is more than a lover to me. By his admission, he calls me his Muse, and he is very much an intellectual companion.

Gesturing towards the book lying next to her: "It was after meeting Voltaire that I began immersing myself in the writings of Newton, whose Principia Mathematica has transformed our understanding of the universe.

It was a simple language task when I started translating Newton's work. However, it evolved into much more, and the concept of universal gravitation made perfect sense to me. I made many discoveries along the way."

What is it like to challenge the conventional wisdom, particularly as a woman in a male-dominated field?"

Émilie sighs and leans back against the tree. "It's a constant battle, and it is true. I am fortunate to have support. Voltaire is a great ally, and so are many philosophers who frequent our home here at Cirey. But the world is not always kind.

My gender is often a hindrance rather than an asset. Still, I never let that stop me. What's more, I know that my ideas can stand on their own."

You are a great deal more than an intellectual, though, Madam. You are a Muse for many vital thinkers. How do you view your role in inspiring others?

A soft smile appears on her lips: "Ah, the idea of being a Muse. I have never set out to be anyone's inspiration. Instead, I am driven by a passion for knowledge and ideas. Still, you are right; I have influenced several men apart from Voltaire.

For example, my conversations with my tutor, Jean le Rond d'Alembert, the great mathematician and philosopher, are invaluable.

Another of my close collaborators is Alexis Clairaut, the prominent mathematician and astronomer who is also one of my tutors. Although our relationship is primarily academic, we are also, as you might say, emotionally close.

While Alexis finds my intellect challenging, I have pushed him to make more outstanding efforts in our shared scientific work.

I enjoy a rich intellectual exchange here at Cirey with several visiting thinkers. All are eager to share ideas and discuss the great questions of existence, knowledge, and nature. This estate has become a small learning centre, a mental refuge.

I love the sharing of ideas and have never regarded my intellect as solely for my gain. I have shared my discoveries and insights freely. What's important is passing on, not hoarding the light of knowledge."

Despite the role you so clearly play as a Muse, inspiring these figures, have your romantic relationships perhaps overshadowed your scientific achievements?

Her expression becomes more serious as she considers my question. "I do not think my relationships should define me, nor should they overshadow my intellectual contributions.

In 1734, Voltaire sought refuge at Cirey to escape arrest due to his controversial writings. With my husband's consent, Voltaire moved into the château, and he and I began a collaborative intellectual partnership.

Voltaire funded extensive renovations at Cirey, including adding a new wing that housed my laboratory and a library containing approximately 21,000 books. This arrangement transformed Cirey into a hub for scientific and philosophical inquiry.

Perhaps it was inevitable that we became lovers. My husband, the Marquis, knew of our liaison. After all, he benefited from the improvements Voltaire financed at Cirey.

He often stayed at the château with me. Yes, I know it was unconventional, but it meant we could pursue our scholarly endeavours with the Marquis's tacit approval."

You may be involved with one of the world's great minds, but you are an inspirer and thinker in your own right, independent and whole.

"Yes, I may inspire men, but more importantly, I inspire ideas. I do not believe one should separate the two. I like to think that my ideas, particularly my work on Newton's theories, will pave the way for tomorrow's physics."

Regardless of these others, Madame, you are certainly one of the key figures shaping the scientific landscape.

"You are kind to say so. True, I was among the first to embrace and expand upon Newton's work, though others have since claimed to have discovered these ideas on their own.

Many are happy to work within the boundaries set by tradition, whether in philosophy, art, or science.

But I believe the boundaries can be pushed, and I intend to push them further. For example, I am fascinated by the mixture of different disciplines and their connections.

My work on the Institutions de Physique, yet to be published, is not just a general treatise on the philosophical nature of physics. Instead, it is a systematic, detailed introduction to the principles of Newtonian physics.

I hope it will become a helpful guide to current physical theories."

You've written extensively, but I wonder to what extent the intellectual landscape is unwelcoming to women.

"I live in a world dominated by men in intellect and expertise, but I have never allowed that to stop me. Women are as capable of deep intellectual work as men are, and I attempt to demonstrate this in my writings and deeds.

I remind people repeatedly that human beings, regardless of gender, absolutely need intellectual affirmation. I always advocate for women's education and point to my translations and commentary to prove that women can think about complex ideas."

Your ability to blend scientific rigour with philosophical exploration sets you apart. How would you like to be remembered?

Her face softens as she gazes out over the garden. "I would like to be remembered as a woman of intellect who pushed the boundaries of thought and inquiry. I do not wish to be remembered for who I loved or was with.

I want my ideas to be the legacy and my work to be seen as a bridge between the past and future, contributing to the excellent knowledge chain stretching across generations."

Can you help me sum up your contributions and role as a Muse?

"Well, I will mainly leave that task for others. However, I want to be remembered for my collaboration with Voltaire, our conduct of scientific experiments, and co-authored essays.

Beyond that, I want people to know I contributed to discussions about the nature of celestial bodies, planetary motion and the laws governing the universe."

And your publications?

"We have touched on my Newtonian physics work, but I have written more broadly than that. For example, my upcoming Institutions de Physique or Foundations of Physics covers the entirety of physics. My translation of Mandeville's Fable of the Bees has criticisms and commentary on how I feel about human behaviour and morality."

Madam, thank you for expressing your views to me this morning. It

has been a delightful and unforgettable privilege.

"I, too, have enjoyed our little encounter and wish you well. I need to attend my laboratory now. I'm using heavy objects to investigate momentum conservation principles and energy transfer in collisions.

I wish you a safe journey; please visit again at some point.

May your world know many more women who ask questions, challenge rules, and dare to write their names into the book of science."

This most impressive woman physicist walks gently away, leaving behind the echo of her intellect and a lingering presence, like a rare vintage, complex, unforgettable, and leaving an aftertaste that lingers in the mind and stirs admiration.

THE MUSE PERSPECTIVE

Émilie du Châtelet inspired mathematicians, philosophers, and scientists by demonstrating that women could master complex ideas and contribute meaningfully to intellectual life.

She was a partner and intellectual equal to Voltaire. It was said that he seduced her as a partner, and she astonished him. She was inspirational to men of letters, scientists, and thinkers of her era.

Émilie attracted admirers and critics. In academia, men often struggled to see her, admiring her intellect and feeling their achievements challenged by her success. As for Voltaire, her love for him was without limit.

While Voltaire often admired Émilie as his Muse, she transcended that traditional role. Her intellectual pursuits were a model to others, and her contributions to science and philosophy firmly established her as an intellectual in her own right.

She translated from Latin to French and commented upon Newton's Principia Mathematica, making a substantial critique and clarification, bringing the work to a broader audience.

She appended an extensive commentary elucidating Newton's ideas, particularly about the laws of motion and gravity. Her work was indicative of the scientific progress of her time.

She also helped establish and refine the modern concept of kinetic energy and made vital contributions. Her idea of kinetic energy was foundational for classical mechanics.

Her work classifying the nature of fire helped establish the energy theory in its early stages through analysis of fire and its association with heat. She claimed that heat was a motion that set the stage for the later development of thermodynamics.

She was a woman of spirit and energy, one of the great minds of the eighteenth-century international network of writers, scholars and philosophers, often called the Republic of Letters.

NOTE: *Daring Genius of the Enlightenment: Émilie du Châtelet, by Judith Zinsser, Penguin Books , is an excellent and engaging biography.*

ADA LOVELACE

1815–1852

Ada Lovelace was a complex and charismatic person with a deep curiosity about the world around her.

As she grew older, she developed a vivid imagination and became a muse to Charles Babbage, mathematician, philosopher, inventor and mechanical engineer.

Ada recognised the potential of Babbage's Analytical Engine beyond mere calculations. Her detailed notes on the engine included an algorithm for its use, making Ada the first person to develop the idea of computer programming.

Her contributions, blending mathematics and creativity, laid the groundwork for modern computing. Yet her work is often overshadowed by others, such as Alan Turing.

ADA LOVELACE

It's the late 1830s, and Ada Lovelace, already gaining a reputation as an extraordinary mind and muse, has agreed to meet me at the British Museum.

This place is already a major institution and a central hub for intellectuals, scholars, and artists. Ada often visits here because of her background in mathematics, science, and the arts.

We meet in one of the museum's private rooms. Her external appearance and demeanour are those of a 19th-century aristocrat. Yet her ideas and intellect make her timeless.

She stands at a crossroads, rooted in the science of her time, while reaching toward a future only she can imagine, one of logic, reason, and the potential of machines."

Good afternoon, Lady Lovelace. It is a distinct honour to speak with you today.

"You are most welcome. Where would you like to begin?"

With your origins, Lady Lovelace. Can you share a little about your early life and how you became so profoundly involved with mathematics and machines?

"Yes, I am happy to do so. But first, please call me Ada. I became Lady Ada upon marriage.

I was born in December 1815 and am the only legitimate child of the poet Lord Byron. My mother was the reformer Anne Isabella Milbanke.

Lord Byron expected his child to be a "glorious boy" and was deeply upset when I turned out to be a girl.

I was named after my father's half-sister, Augusta Leigh. Byron himself named me Ada, but I had no connection with my famous, some say, notorious father, who died when I was eight.

Believe it or not, I was not shown the family portrait of my father until my 20th birthday.

My father, a poet of considerable fame, was a tempestuous man, but my mother, Lady Byron, was entirely different. She was keenly interested in mathematics as an intellectual and saw my father's poetic side as unstable.

She was determined to steer me away from that side of my background and ensured that I inherited a love for numbers and logic.

My mother believed the best way to counterbalance my father's volatile and passionate nature was to encourage a disciplined, logical mind. So, from a very young age, I was educated in the mathematical sciences.

My childhood life in London was quiet and studious. I was often at home learning mathematics, languages, and music from private tutors.

Despite my mother's rigid requirements, I was naturally curious and had access to a great variety of books.

I've been studying with Augustus De Morgan - you may have heard of him? He's the mathematics professor at University College London. His ideas on algebra and logic are pretty ahead of their time.

This early exposure to intellectual pursuits has laid the foundation for my current and future work."

De Morgan demonstrated his profound respect for your intellectual

capacity and ability to grasp complex mathematical concepts.

"It's kind of you to say that since our relationship has mainly been teacher-student. However, I believe he has felt inspired by my enthusiasm for mathematics and my determination to engage with new ideas.

I would even assert that I influenced his thinking about logic and algebra.

Then, I was introduced to Charles Babbage, who would become one of the most influential figures in my life. My mother's vision for me was indeed unique for the time.

She encouraged me to engage with complex, intellectual subjects rather than conform to the expectations placed on women.

When I was 20, in 1835, I married William King, who became the 7th Baron King upon his father's passing, and he inherited the title.

We now live at Ockham Park, a large and elegant estate in Surrey, just outside London. This is our main residence, where we've raised our family of three children.

Though I greatly respect William's intelligence and do my best to support his career in the British Aristocracy, our marriage has its challenges.

With William often away, I find myself isolated, and my health is not as good as I would wish. William is supportive and provides me with stability and social standing.

Yet my social position means that married life is less helpful for the intensive, exploratory research I did in the early days."

I gather that Ockham Park is a beautiful, secluded estate with

lovely grounds, gardens, and a grand house.

"That's true. I value its quietness and privacy for reflection and study, which allow me to pursue my intellectual interests. But we also host social gatherings there, and I have been able to collaborate with intellectuals, scientists, and mathematicians."

You spoke of Babbage; how did you first encounter him?

"I first met the talented British mathematician Charles Babbage when I was seventeen. My mother and I attended one of his Saturday night soirées with my mutual friend and private tutor, Mary Somerville.

These were social gatherings in Babbage's home, held regularly, typically once a week, on Saturday evenings. They were invaluable for me."

Please tell me more about them.

"The gatherings were well-known for stimulating discussions on mathematics, science, philosophy, and technology.

Some of the most distinguished figures of our era attended, such as Michael Faraday, the pioneering experimental scientist best known for his work in electromagnetism.

Others I met included Sir George Everest, the British surveyor and geographer and Henry Thomas Colebrooke, a British scholar renowned for his work on Indian mathematics and Sanskrit."

What were these soirées like, Ada?

"Though they appeared casual on the surface, they were in truth lively gatherings of sharp minds. Ideas - scientific, mathematical, philosophical - were exchanged and contested with great energy.

Mr. Babbage, in particular, seldom missed an opportunity to speak of his engines.

He was tireless in demonstrating the Difference Engine to any who would listen, and he often hinted at an even greater ambition - the Analytical Engine, a machine not yet built, but fully alive in his imagination."

Can you talk more about Babbage? What is he like?

"Babbage affectionately calls me 'Lady Fairy.' Funnily enough, when I was about thirteen, I dreamed of flying like a fairy. I constructed wings of various materials and studied birds to learn the proportion between wings and bodies.

I even wrote a little illustrated volume, which I called Flyology, recording my findings.

But of course, you asked about Mr. Babbage. He is, in many ways, a kindred spirit - an inspiring, if complex, man with a mind of astonishing reach.

I was already drawn to mechanical inventions when I first heard of his Difference Engine.

Imagine a mechanical apparatus designed to calculate mathematical tables with precision and reliability. That first meeting revealed to me the true breadth of Mr. Babbage's ambitions.

Not content with the Difference Engine alone, he soon conceived of something even more extraordinary - the Analytical Engine.

A machine that, in principle, could perform any series of operations according to the instructions it receives.

I found this vision utterly captivating. While Mr. Babbage worked to bring the machine into being, he also sought minds who might help him explore its deeper potential. That was when my involvement truly began to deepen.

I had long been immersed in the principles of mathematics, and I found that I could contribute in ways few others could. We began a correspondence that has already endured for many years, and I believe the best of it is yet to come."

Is your collaboration with Babbage vital to the development of your own ideas?

"Yes, in several ways. Mr. Babbage's designs - particularly his notions of mechanical calculation - provided me with a structure, a starting place, if you will.

But it was never enough for me to admire the machinery. I was drawn to what lay beyond the mechanism itself. His engines stirred in me the sense that such a device could be far more than a machine for numerical calculation alone.

I began to imagine how symbols, not merely quantities, might be manipulated - how the engine, if rightly instructed, could perform operations of remarkable generality.

I have often called this 'poetical science' - the marriage of reason and imagination.

It is not the machine alone that fascinates me, but the larger principle it suggests: that human thought itself might be mirrored, extended, or even transformed through mechanical means.

Mr. Babbage laid the groundwork, but I have sought to build upon it a vision that reaches farther than either of us first imagined.

Second, he asked me to translate an article by an Italian

mathematician, Luigi Federico Menabrea, who wrote a French paper about Babbage's Analytical Engine in 1842.

My translation included extensive notes and my vision of the machine's potential."

Could you explain those notes and your understanding of the machine's capabilities?

"As I worked through the translation, I found I had so much to add and many insights about the machine's potential. I was not content merely to translate the article; I wanted to contribute my own thoughts as well. And so, my notes expanded well beyond what the Italian had written.

In my additions, "Notes by the Translator," I described the Analytical Engine as a calculator and something far more profound.

I suggested that it could repeat instructions, enabling it to perform complex tasks and would be able to weave algebraic patterns, just as the Jacquard loom weaves flowers and leaves."

Would you say that your role in Babbage's work was primarily as a collaborator, or do you view yourself more as a muse for his creativity?

"That's an interesting question. I often joke about my role in Babbage's work. Yes, you are correct; I act as his muse. He is brilliant, but like many great minds, he can get lost in the details and lose sight of the facts.

I can see the machine's possibilities and envision what it could grow into. He is often mired in the quirks of its building.

I don't want to minimise my contributions as I am not just a passive muse.

I bring a deep understanding of mathematical knowledge and innovative approaches to thinking about abstract concepts. But yes, my job is to help communicate the full breadth of Babbage's agenda.

I push him hard to think bigger and to envision how much the world could change with such a machine, rather than becoming distracted by the act of building it.

You could say that, in many ways, my work is ahead of its time. But while I am well-regarded in some circles, my ideas have not been widely appreciated.

The world of mathematics and science remains very much dominated by men. Women with the intellectual capabilities to make significant contributions are often dismissed or overlooked.

Many of my contemporaries don't fully understand my writings on the Analytical Engine. Babbage's machine, though revolutionary, remains incomplete.

So, my vision of the future has not yet been realised. That's how things go in life sometimes, and I live with that."

Can you describe the specific challenges or societal expectations you encounter as a woman involved in mathematics and science?

"What a question. I could go on about these issues all day. Right now, there are rigid gender roles that restrict women's participation in intellectual pursuits.

Those limitations are particularly relevant in the fields of mathematics and technology. Today, these are considered male preserves.

Of course, a few of my contemporaries and I push against obstacles, such as our primary domestic roles of marrying, raising children, and supporting our husbands.

In that respect, I do the best I can. However, we're not expected to engage in public, intellectual, or scientific arenas.

Women's education primarily focuses on the arts, languages, and social skills. Higher education and intellectual careers are generally off-limits to women.

So naturally, you haven't attended university or any formal scientific institutions?

"Yes, you're correct. Yet, I'm a scientist and consider myself to have technical knowledge. However, I'm often seen as an 'amateur' or a 'lady' in the serious scientific inquiry world.

As a young girl, I was told that my interests in mathematics and machines were not typical of women of my time, and I encountered resistance from all sides.

However, I did not let that discourage me. I had faith in the power of the mind and the importance of curiosity.

Never let your gender or anyone else's expectations define your destiny. Passion and perseverance are mightier than prejudice.

It's been an honour to hear your story and reflect on your contributions to science, technology, and our understanding of machines' potential.

"Well, thank you, too. It's been a pleasure to share my thoughts, and I hope the future holds even more remarkable possibilities for those willing to dream and create.

I have always believed that the Analytical Engine is not just a machine for calculation but a precursor to the ones that will eventually shape our world."

THE MUSE PERSPECTIVE

Ada Lovelace influenced generations of innovators, mathematicians, and creative thinkers, particularly those who operate in the grey zones between categories that seem far apart, like science and the arts.

During her lifetime, her distinct method of extending mathematics through imagination resonated with individuals whose work was at the forefront of emerging technologies, including Charles Babbage.

He valued her technical observations about his Analytical Engine.

Many years after Lovelace died at 36, her legacy finally took hold, and her status as a marvellous muse took root.

Her history has inspired people to explore the boundaries of what is possible and re-examine the nature of technology in human life.

Despite her early death, her work indirectly inspired later figures in computer science, such as Alan Turing. Yet, he, too, built upon ideas that Lovelace proposed more than a century earlier.

In a sense, Turing formalised the idea of computation that Lovelace had anticipated. Similarly, Ada and her story inspired others and indirectly encouraged their later groundbreaking achievements in the 20th century.

Her legacy reminds us that imagination is as vital as logic in shaping the future of technology.

NOTE: You may enjoy Ada's Algorithm: How Ada Lovelace, Lord Byron's Daughter, Launched the Digital Age Through the Poetry of Numbers by James Essinger, Nov 2016

See also: Ada Lovelace, Britanica https://www.britannica.com/biography/Ada-Lovelace

JANE MORRIS

1839-1914

Jane Morris offers a candid reflection on her life as a Muse within the Pre-Raphaelite Brotherhood, sharing her transformation from an unknown working-class girl into an enduring icon of art and independence.

She offers a rare glimpse into the sacrifices and activities behind the admired works that have earned her a reputation for inspiring others.

Her enduring influence and legacy as a strong, confident woman stemmed from her refusal to be subordinate to men.

JANE MORRIS

It's the mid-1870s, and I'm meeting Jane in the drawing room of her charming home, Kelmscott Manor, in Oxfordshire.

This place reflects its rural surroundings with traditional Cotswold stone architecture, gabled roofs, and lattice-like windows.

William Morris and Dante Gabriel Rossetti have jointly leased the property as a retreat, a place of solace and inspiration for their artistic pursuits.

Tapestries, handcrafted furniture, and textiles designed by William Morris fill this quiet, elegant space. A large window casts natural light, giving the room a serene ambience.

Jane sits in an upholstered chair by the hearth, working on her embroidery. This setting reflects her cultivated taste and her active participation in the Arts and Crafts Movement.

It also offers a private space where she can speak candidly with me about her life and experiences as a Muse.

Gesturing to a chair on the other side of the hearth, she offers a welcoming smile.

"You want to talk about being a Muse, I believe."

Yes, I'm on a mission to explore the role of the Muse and how it unfolds.

"For me, it all began quite unexpectedly. I was merely Jane Burden, a working-class girl from Oxford, poor, uneducated, and with little notion of what the world held for me.

My life changed when I went to the Oxford Theatre with my sister in

1857. The theatre was a unique venue where people like me could meet others from different classes.

Dante Gabriel Rossetti, Edward Burne-Jones and Ned, a friend of theirs, spotted me in the theatre crowds.

They approached me and asked if I would 'sit' for them. At first, I was defensive as I didn't understand what they meant.

But they seemed respectable and claimed to see something in me, though I had no idea what it was.

They gave me an address to visit the next day, but my mother forbade me from going, as there had been no proper introduction.

By chance, we met Ned on the street a few days later, and he asked why I hadn't come to their studio. I explained about my mother's concern.

Everything was sorted, and I went to their studio to do some posing.

It was a whole lot better paid and less tiring than washing clothes, scrubbing steps or scouring pots.

Rossetti raved about how beautiful I was. No one had ever told me that. It felt suspended between disbelief and possibilities.

For Rossetti, I was a living embodiment of mythic and literary women - Guinevere, Proserpine, and Beatrice.

His obsession with myth and idealising women often meant I ceased to be myself. It was a difficult adjustment at first.

Imagine being transformed into something so far removed from the reality of who you are. Yet, I understood it as his art, his way of making sense of the world."

Can you explain why Rossetti and your future husband, William Morris, chose you as a model for their art?

"It's a good question, but the answer is quite simple.

Both were working on murals for the Oxford Union building when they spotted me at the theatre.

They and their fellow artists, often referred to as the Pre-Raphaelite Brotherhood, were fascinated with what they called "authentic" beauty.

Usually, they looked for women who were natural models and not from the upper classes, which I was not. They idealised certain physical traits associated with a medieval or romantic aesthetic, which they believed I embodied."

Jane hesitates and runs her fingers over the embroidery, an art she has perfected under William's tutelage:

"If I were a Muse during this period, Rossetti was the first to direct me towards becoming a new person.

I wasn't a subject to him but a reflection of his vision."

How did that translate into his art?

"When Rossetti painted me, he expressed his ideals of love, transformation and moral struggles.

For William, I played a different role. My natural judgment and ability to contribute something meaningful to his work allowed him to bring me into the fold.

Initially, I was not drawn to William. Even so, he compulsively drew me, and gradually, I got to know him better.

When he proposed, I was stunned. It was an offer beyond my dreams for a working-class girl like me. I spent the next year preparing to become a lady.

I learned about manners, etiquette, and household management. My reading and writing were polished, and I became William's partner in creating the life and art he envisioned.

After we married, my embroidery was a craft I took up under his guidance. By then, though, I was also deeply in love with Gabriel Rossetti.

He and his best friend, my husband, bought Kelmscott. This meant that Gabriel and I could spend significant time here without it attracting too much attention."

Jane, how could Morris and Rossetti afford this country retreat, and are Muses supposed to fall in love with their protégé?

William's design business is thriving, and a few years back, moved to Queen Square. It's now widely recognised for its wallpapers, textiles, and stained glass and has important clients among churches, country houses, and the artistic circles of London.

Meanwhile, Gabriel's paintings attract considerable attention and sell fast. As for my feelings for him, what do you expect?

He's charming, attentive and passionate, while William is often grumpy and distracted by his growing business.

I have never given myself entirely to Gabriel since he suffers awful guilt over the death of his wife. He was also concerned that he was betraying his best friend.

With all the worry, poor Gabriel partially lost his eyesight and temporarily had to stop painting. Our time together, though, has been highly productive, a period of intense artistic output by Gabriel.

As his Muse, I have encouraged him to return to painting, and he has since done some of his best work.

This place is the perfect setting to accommodate and nurture Gabriel's themes of myths and melancholia, often using me as the central figure."

What was your husband's attitude to your affair with Rossetti?

"He knows of it but chooses to ignore it, and often travels. His primary focus has always been on creative endeavours and community engagement.

His contributions to art, literature, and design define his life more than the complexities of his private relationships.

You also have two children, Jenny and May, with your husband, William.

"Yes, Jenny showed an early aptitude for learning and is now studying at Oxford. May was born in 1862, and it's too early to say how she'll develop, but the signs are good.

Maybe she'll do something in the Arts and Crafts movement, perhaps even take over William's firm. Who knows?"

How have others in your circle and families reacted to your prominent role as a Muse?

Jane sighs and shakes her head. "I am often regarded as an enigma.

Since my origins were no secret, people have found it peculiar, even unsettling, that a stableman's daughter could ascend into the circles of Rossetti, Morris, and Burne-Jones.

Some admired me; others pitied or resented me. Women, especially, seem to have conflicting feelings about me.

To some, I'm a potent symbol of transformation. But to others, I am merely a victim of men's whims and the male desire that seeks idealised possession."

A shadow crosses her placid face. "As for myself, I feel torn. Being a Muse is not always flattering. It is to be looked at and used for another's vision, rarely understood as its own.

"There is power in it, but also a loss of self and individuality. For all his declared passion and painterly attention, Gabriel does not honestly know me as Jane. To him, I am a symbol.

Only William, I think, sees me as a whole person, though even he cannot escape his idealisations. There are moments, however, when I find joy in being part of something larger.

For instance, Gabriel's painting 'Proserpine' captured something about longing and entrapment that resonated deeply with me. Perhaps it was her story and my own that he painted."

How has your role as a Muse evolved?

"Mmm, in the early days, I was passive, a silent figure to be painted, admired, and mythologised.

Gradually, I began to find my voice and not just as a model. I have become someone who contributes ideas and opinions and corresponds with figures like Bernard Shaw.

With William, I learned that my perspective has value. My role in his life is not confined to inspiration. It extends to practical work, whether managing household affairs, hosting his friends, or embroidering designs.

At the same time, I have moved from a model to someone with influence in my own right. Being a Muse means different things to different artists.

To Rossetti, I was an ideal; to William, a collaborator; to Burne-Jones, an echo of a bygone age. For me, it is a journey of self-discovery."

THE MUSE PERSPECTIVE

Jane Morris's life as a Muse was like a dance, combining personal identity with artistic idealisation.

Born into poverty, she became one of the most recognisable figures of the Pre-Raphaelite movement. This movement sought to return to what they perceived as the purer, more sincere, and detailed art that preceded Raphael's influence.

Jane's early role as Rossetti's Muse was indeed one of passivity. Her striking beauty became synonymous with the Brotherhood's vision of womanhood.

Over time, however, she grew into a more active and collaborative role, particularly alongside her husband, William Morris, whose poetic, design and business endeavours she supported as a Muse and partner.

Despite Jane's affair with Dante Gabriel Rossetti, Jane's marriage to William lasted, although it was never conventionally romantic.

Jane and William remained partners in a deep intellectual and familial sense. After her husband died in the early 1890s, Jane assumed a significant role in managing his legacy, and their daughter, May, took over from her.

Jane was a Muse but resisted being reduced to a mere symbol, and she had creative partnerships with many artists.

Most works featuring Jane are housed in prominent repositories, ranging from the Tate Britain in London to the Birmingham Museum and Art Gallery and the Delaware Art Museum in the United States.

The artworks Jane inspired continue to resonate with viewers, conveying mythology, romance, and medieval themes. Her presence reminds us how the line between inspiration and identity can blur, making the Muse both exalted and unseen.

NOTE: For more about Jane, there's the well-written biography of mother and daughter in Jane and May Morris, by Jan Marsh, Pandora, 1986.

CAMILLE CLAUDEL

1864 – 1943

Camille Claudel was an intense and unforgettable force - a woman of vision, defiance, and haunting artistry.

Her sculptural work thrums with strength and fragility. She was an artist herself, not just a muse to others.

In defiance of Rodin's looming shadow, Camille's legacy echoes far beyond it, speaking through her art.

CAMILLE CLAUDEL

"Welcome to my studio," Camille says softly yet firmly.

"This is where I find my authentic self. Away from expectations, away from judgments. Here, I can be free.

"Is it true you are here to speak with me about the role of Muse?"

Yes, Madamoiselle. Thank you for sparing the time to do that.

This room embodies the essence of her work: beautiful and haunting sculptures, such as The Age of Maturity, which is still in progress.

There is also the emotional Sakountala, depicting a young couple with a kneeling man embracing a woman who leans towards him. It's a flowing structure and one of Camille's most admired and recognised masterpieces.

The studio walls are lined with her other sculptures, silent witnesses to her successes and ultimate heartbreak.

She wipes her hands as she puts down some clay, which she will soon return to shaping:

"I am known as a muse to others, but I am also an artist in my own right. I do not need anyone to define me, nor to limit me."

I hear that, Mademoiselle. Could you tell me something about your early life, your artistic journey, and how you chose sculpture to express your strong feelings about life?

"My journey began in 1864 when I was born in Fère-en-Tardenois, a small village in northern France. The Sisters of Christian Doctrine taught me until I was twelve, and when our family moved to Nogent-sur-Seine, my education continued with a tutor.

After that, I had little formal education but read widely. Luckily, my father had a well-stocked library and a high-powered job in the French Ministry of Finance.

He was a man of strict principles, deeply rooted in his traditional views, and believed that a woman's place was in the home, not pursuing a career."

How did he react to your desire to be a sculptor?

"He disapproved and dismissed my passion as a frivolous and unsuitable ambition for a woman. Being so conventional, he wanted me to focus on more traditional pursuits, such as marriage and motherhood.

Over time, his attitude grew colder and more distant. I think it was because he could neither understand nor accept my determination to follow my artistic path.

When he was transferred to Paris and the family moved there, I became within reach of a beacon of hope for someone like me.

The Colarossi Academy was one of the few places that accepted women, but even then, it was rare. Through sheer determination and resourcefulness, I managed to gain entry."

It must have been a struggle.

"As you say, it was a battle to secure the necessary support. But my belief in my talent pushed me forward.

Once accepted into the Academy, I knew I had to work harder than ever to prove that I could succeed, regardless of the barriers my father and society had placed in my way."

Is that when you met your mentor, Auguste Rodin?

"Yes, around 1883 and also my lifelong friend Jessie Lipscomb.

She was a sister in spirit and someone who truly understood me. At the Academy, we navigated the challenges of being female sculptors in a male-dominated world.

From the moment we met, there was an immediate connection. We shared our artistic passion and forged a bond of mutual support. Jessie was different from the other students. Like me, she was bold, independent, and energetic.

In many ways, I acted as Jessie's muse. I strengthened her artistic voice, persuaded her to trust her intuition, and, above all, helped her believe in her own power. From me, she learned how to stand firm despite facing criticism.

Meanwhile, I, too, gained from her calming presence, which helped me navigate sometimes overwhelming self-doubt.

Put simply, Jessie helped settle me emotionally. Jessie offered an invaluable perspective when things got complicated, particularly with family or the turmoil surrounding Rodin.

We were each other's support system, and our friendship grew more profound over the years. We also left a lasting mark on one another's work. Jessie provided a fresh lens for viewing my art."

I can see that she was so essential to you.

"Yes, it was a partnership that kept me going, and I cherished her for it."

Can you tell me about your time at the Academy? It must have been an exciting and fulfilling experience.

"In such a place, I naturally met some of the most important figures in the Parisian art world, including Auguste Rodin.

It is no secret that apart from a close working relationship, I became his pupil, lover, and muse.

Our relationship has been one of passion, creativity, and tension, but also the beginning of a complicated, often painful chapter in my life."

If it's not too painful, Mademoiselle, could you briefly discuss this critical time?

"Rodin changed my life, but has also held me back." Her eyes brim with emotion.

Even so, you have not faded into the background and become invisible, have you?

"Certainly not! My work is beginning to acquire its distinct voice. Raw emotion and depth fill my being and transfer directly to my work.

For example, I have created La Valse, depicting two lovers locked in a passionate yet tragic embrace."

Ah, La Valse. How did that wonderful piece come to be?

"The doors of the École des Beaux-Arts were firmly shut to women like me. Denied the education and connections it offered, I have sought another path, turning directly to the state institutions that fund public art.

But those institutions, how they clung to their old ways! They favour male artists, their chosen sons groomed within the walls of the École.

Still, I dared to propose La Valse. It embodies music and motion and is bold yet born from my passion and vision. It is a swirling dance captured in stone. Although the technical challenges were immense, I knew I could meet them.

But the inspector and the gatekeepers of the state institutions found fault. 'Too naked,' they said as if art could not be both sensual and sublime!

They have refused to fund it, denying me the chance to show my work to the public and to take my rightful place among the greats."

La Valse is more than stone - it is the cry of a soul demanding to be seen.

"Yes, it symbolises my struggle to create and be seen and heard in a world that prefers my silence. I have reworked the piece several times, first with draperies and finally a third version with fewer draperies.

My efforts have not been enough to allow the project to proceed. Despite my adjustments, the project has still failed to please the sponsors."

You must feel devastated.

"You're right; I was and am still in a state of shock. It marks an essential moment in my fight to be taken seriously as an artist. This painful experience has strengthened my determination to continue creating art on my own terms.

Without support from official channels or patrons?

"None. I keep seeking private funding. For instance, I received financial backing from Countess de Maigret, who admires my work. This has enabled me to complete the piece on my terms.

Around this time, I also created a sculpture that portrayed the destructive nature of gossip, jealousy, and societal pressure.

I am determined to break free from these constraints, but the world around me, especially Rodin, refuses to let me fully step into the light."

These wonderful works are not just sculptures, Mademoiselle. They undeniably reveal your emotional turmoil and determination to resist the confines of societal expectations.

"Indeed, they do, Monsieur. You see, Rodin is both my teacher and my burden. He taught me so much about the form of the human body, but he also controls the expression of our relationship.

It is hard to fight for my identity when the world sees us as a unit - Rodin and Claudel, never just me."

Yet it is no exaggeration to say that Rodin, under your influence, has created masterpieces such as The Kiss and The Thinker.

"You are correct. His art is starting to resemble some of my ideas distinctly.

For instance, the emotional intensity in his figures owes much to our working relationship. People may not always recognise it, but some of my ideas and methods are reflected in his work.

I may be his muse, but I am also a creator in my own right."

In 1893, Mademoiselle, you opened your studio here in Paris. Was this a new beginning?

"Yes, a new phase of being an independent artist. I have begun creating works that reflect my struggles, including "The Broken Jug" and "The Hand of God."

I am trying to find my distinct voice, one that is separate from Rodin's influence.

My break with Rodin has become permanent. I am focusing only on my artistic vision and continue to explore themes of tension and release, often dealing with the internal struggles of the human psyche.

I am also starting to experiment with bronze casting."

Your role as a muse is well recognised and not restricted to just Rodin.

"No, you're correct there, too. My role as a muse extends beyond Rodin to my brother, Paul Claudel, the famous poet and diplomat.

I continually hope that my work will give him courage, that my art will urge him toward the light, and that, in some way, I might be a good angel to him.

Although Paul often acknowledges me as a source of inspiration, he increasingly distances himself from me.

Like my father, he cannot fully understand my independent, rebellious nature. Paul sees me as a problem, a burden, a tragedy. He has never accepted my way of life and my choices."

Apart from Rodin and your brother, your influence as a muse goes far wider.

"True. I had a brief romantic relationship with the prominent sculptor Jean-Baptiste Auguste Clésinger.

He's an artist who lives in the shadows of convention. Although we share an intellectual bond, his vision is more traditional in nature.

As a muse, I give him a sense of what art could be. But he always fears straying too far from the established norms.

You see, I am not just a muse in the way people imagine - silent, pliant, and present to inspire without contributing.

My presence, ideas, movements, and doubts become part of the clay I shape. For Clésinger, I am not just a model but a force, someone whose energy and spirit demand his work rise to meet it.

Being a muse is no passive role. To be on the receiving end can be intoxicating, even overwhelming. I mirror Clésinger's ambitions and insecurities.

My pursuit of sculpture may challenge and even unsettle him. I am never content to be merely the muse, a source of beauty or emotion that an artist seeks to capture. I also want to create and transform."

You are both his inspiration and his torment.

"Exactly. I push him to see the boundaries of his artistry. What he sees in me, I hope, is more than the form he admires. It is part of the fire that drives us to create, even when it consumes us."

Mademoiselle, I have much enjoyed our conversation. You have been marvellously frank about your life. Thank you for sharing some of your life story with such willingness.

"Now I return to my clay - where silence breaks, and my spirit takes shape again."

THE MUSE PERSPECTIVE

Camille Claudel never entirely escaped Rodin's shadow, which shaped her work.

But both La Valse and The Gossips advertised her brilliance and individuality. Together, these works influenced artists like Aristide Maillol and even contemporary sculptors.

Her work also profoundly impacted the views of women artists who followed later.

Though her art was often dismissed, her genius could not be buried. Camille's voice, carved in bronze and anguish, still calls to those who dare to create.

She continued to exhibit at recognised salons, though, just as often, she would utterly destroy every piece of work in her studio.

Camille became obsessed with Rodin's injustice to her, hogging the limelight she felt belonged to her. She began to feel persecuted by him and his "gang".

Alienated from most of human society, she lived far from Paul, her only family member close to her.

She struggled with financial difficulties and sometimes wandered the streets in rags.

She was finally overwhelmed by her condition and, in 1913, was involuntarily committed to an asylum until her death three decades later.

NOTE: There are no current English biographies of Camille.

You may find a used edition of "Camille: The Life of Camille Claudel, Rodin's Muse and Mistress" by Reine-Marie, published by Henry Holt & Co in 1988.

Check out the National Museum of Women in the Arts: Camille Claudel, and Britannica: https://www.britannica.com/biography/Camille-Claudel

ALBERT SCHWEITZER

1875 – 1965

Albert Schweitzer was a musician, theologian, physician, and one of the 20th century's great humanitarians.

His "Reverence for Life" philosophy stresses the inherent worth of all living beings. This has influenced the thinking and actions of individuals such as Albert Einstein, Martin Luther King Jr., and Nelson Mandela, leading them towards service and social justice.

His work in running a hospital in harsh conditions in Gabon was exemplary and attracted interest from around the world.

Although the world was not surprised, Schweitzer was astonished to receive the Nobel Peace Prize.

ALBERT SCHWEITZER

It is 1954, and I'm with Dr Albert Schweitzer, the distinguished physician and theologian, at his hospital in Lambaréné, Gabon. The air is thick with the scent of rain and the distant calls of unseen creatures.

We're about to sit together for a conversation on a worn wooden bench overlooking the Ogooué River. In the background, the constant sounds of the African bush are audible.

His hospital in Lambaréné is more of a place to stay while awaiting medical attention than a traditional hospital.

But Schweitzer personally crafted it, and when a more modern one replaced the old one after the Doctor's death, it began to fail.

The legendary Doctor is now in his late 70s, physically robust and spiritually radiant. His tall, lean frame is slightly stooped after years of labouring in Gabon's harsh conditions.

His simple attire consists of a well-worn white linen shirt and khaki trousers, befitting someone devoted to service rather than personal comfort.

Behind him, in his modest surroundings, I spot reminders of his varied life: a well-used piano in one corner, a bookshelf filled with texts on theology, philosophy, and music, and a small, framed picture of his beloved organ in Günsbach.

Schweitzer is a man of action, deep intellect, and artistry. He is a thinker, a healer, and, above all, a servant of humanity.

Just before starting our conversation, I snatch a brief moment to examine the face of this most renowned Muse.

He fixes me with a penetrating gaze. His famous thick moustache, now almost entirely white, twitches slightly as he prepares to speak, lending an air of gravitas to what is to come.

Large, calloused hands from years of manual work in the African jungle rest lightly on his knees. There's something profoundly welcoming and approachable about him.

Doctor Schweitzer, thank you for agreeing to speak with me today. I'm here because your life and work inspire countless individuals worldwide, and I'm keen to hear directly from you about your life's journey.

"You are most welcome. I appreciate you coming all this way to see me. It will be a pleasure to share some thoughts about my work."

Doctor, your Reverence for Life is a remarkable philosophy for which you have earned global acclaim. As this principle guides your actions, can you elaborate on it?

"Indeed, my philosophy of Reverence for Life is a duty. Hopefully, it inspires people to act ethically and with kindness towards others. It asks people to make two essential choices.

First, consider the impact of one's actions on the natural world.

Second, realise the innate essence of every living being, from the smallest insect to the human being. It's about seeing the same spirit in all of life and developing a respect for its sacredness.

This philosophy ultimately informs my work here in Lambaréné, where we attempt to relieve suffering and treat each patient with dignity and compassion."

Can we start with your early life and discuss your family and upbringing?

"Yes, let's see. Well, I was born in Kaysersberg, Germany, in the year 1875. My father, Louis, a Lutheran pastor, naturally influenced my early religious upbringing.

Shortly after my birth, my father was appointed to a parish in Gunsbach, a small village in the Munster Valley, where he served for many years.

That place holds a great deal of significance for me, as I grew up there and developed my early interests. Its serene rural setting grew my love for nature, philosophy, and music. Whenever possible, I like to return to it."

Am I correct that exposure to your father's pastoral duties directly contributed to your humanitarian and spiritual outlook?

"Absolutely. After secondary school, I studied in Strasbourg, earning a doctorate in philosophy and a teaching license in religion.

Meanwhile, I also pursued my passion for music by studying with the renowned Paris organist, Charles-Marie Widor. I also began honing my musical and writing talents on the composer Bach.

For a while, I toured, giving organ recitals at numerous European concerts while earning money to support my education and, later, medical studies.

In 1901, at the age of 26, I was appointed principal of a theological college in Strasbourg. But only a few years later, I dedicated my life to medical missionary work in Africa."

Sometimes, the doctor punctuates his reflections with a soft smile or a self-deprecating chuckle. This endearing habit, in turn, uncovers a man who, despite his gargantuan triumphs, is heartwarming and compassionate.

That was a dramatic career change. How did it happen, and how did you pursue that?

"That's a fair question. It was like this. One day, I came across a missionary journal that listed a brief description of the medical needs in French Equatorial Africa.

After reading about the situation, I couldn't ignore its human implications. It was then that I felt compelled to meet the needs of others.

As you say, it was a dramatic revelation. By then, I was a well-established theologian, musician, and scholar.

Still, I began medical studies and later graduated as a medical doctor at the University of Strasbourg in 1911.

At that point, I was now equipped to serve as a spiritual and medical caregiver."

It must have been hard for you to sacrifice personal comfort and prestige to serve humanity.

"Not just for me, my wife Helene too. She was a trained nurse, and we travelled together to Gabon, where we established a hospital to care for the sick and marginalised.

We began modestly with very basic facilities, but with God's help, the hospital grew to offer a wide range of medical services. Yes, it meant working under challenging conditions, often using my own funds to sustain the mission.

When the First World War began taking its dreadful toll, both Helene and I were eventually interned as German Nationals in a French camp near the Pyrenees for a year in 1917.

After the war ended, we stayed in Europe, where I resumed lecturing and writing. I also gave organ recitals to raise funds for my African hospital.

I returned to Lambaréné in 1924 and rebuilt and expanded my hospital despite the challenges brought on by the Great Depression."

You also remained there right through the Second World War. How on earth did you manage to keep such an extensive operation going in the jungle during wartime, Doctor?

"Well, as I said then, mosquitoes respect no borders.

I continued reminding everyone of the universality of suffering and the need for care.

As a German national working in a French colony, I was in a precarious position. The hospital faced severe shortages of medicine, food, and essential supplies.

I made the best use of local resources and relied on the ingenuity of my staff to keep the hospital running smoothly. It remained a place where my Reverence for Life philosophy prevailed.

There was a wonderful sense of community spirit, and the hospital staff and residents grew even closer during this time. I tried to foster a spirit of unity and shared purpose, enabling us to endure shortages and isolation together."

This brings me to an important issue I want to understand better. Music and medicine are so central in your life. How do you reconcile these contrasting interests?

"Music and medicine are expressions of my deepest values. Music allows me to connect with the sacred and delve into the rawness of humanity and the enigmas of existence.

It doesn't depend on language and culture but speaks to the soul. It is an indirect way of serving humanity, alleviating suffering and enhancing the quality of life for those in need.

My involvement in music and medicine enables me to share my love for life and my dedication to positively impacting the world through the power of music and the pursuit of creating a fulfilling life.

These two pursuits feed each other, enhancing my life and illuminating humanity's condition.

The people here have tremendous needs and great suffering. I have a profound moral responsibility to alleviate their suffering and enhance their quality of life.

It is rewarding in a deeply sustaining way to see the positive impact of our work, no matter how small."

You were awarded the Nobel Prize a couple of years ago. Albert Einstein said, *To know Albert Schweitzer is to understand the best humanity has to offer.* **How do you respond to such recognition?**

"I am deeply humbled by the words of such a great mind. I once had the pleasure of meeting Einstein, and we even played some Bach together, which had a profound impact on both of us.

My goal has always been to live a life of purpose and make a positive contribution to the world. We are each responsible for using our talents and resources to make a difference, alleviate suffering and create a more just and compassionate world.

If my life can inspire others to live with compassion and serve humanity, then my efforts have been worthwhile."

You have been a Muse and influenced many distinguished people, including Einstein. How do you feel about this role and its impact

on those affected?

"You are most kind to call me a Muse, which I humbly accept. My life is partly about influencing as many people as possible through my philosophy. It's challenging to know where to begin regarding specific individuals.

For example, Martin Luther King Jr. drew inspiration from my philosophy of nonviolence for his dedication to social justice. These ideas are now part of his struggle for civil rights.

Nelson Mandela, too, has kindly said that I have deeply influenced him, stating that I am a source of strength and resilience during his years of imprisonment.

Gandhi, too, explicitly acknowledges the resonance of my philosophy with his own in his autobiography. In Reverence for Life, he saw a powerful affirmation of his principles of nonviolent resistance.

This inspired him to advocate for animal and human rights, recognising the interconnectedness of all life.

Gandhi told his followers: '*Here is a man who builds hospitals not just for bodies but for souls; let us learn from him.*'

I am grateful and much humbled by such public affirmations."

Your legacy continues influencing how we think about ethics, the environment, and our shared humanity.

"I am always glad to hear these stories of how my life and philosophy inspire. But I do not claim to be the sole Muse to these people. "

Yes, but many writers and artists have experienced you as their Muse.

"Well, when it comes to writers, I suppose I know of Romain Rolland, the French novelist and Nobel laureate, who has stated that he was inspired by the commitment to universal harmony and used this in his writings.

Another writer I respect, Herman Hesse, did much the same. He, too, discussed achieving a similar balance of spirituality, intellect, and practical engagement in his memorable novel, The Glass Bead Game.

Incidentally, Romain Rolland, the French dramatist, novelist, essayist, art historian kindly visited me in Lambaréné about four years ago."

And what was his reaction, Doctor?

"He admired the simplicity of what we do here. It is so basic in how we treat people as human beings. He also particularly liked that I often play Bach to my patients in the evenings. I explained to him that I believe music has healing power."

Yes, Rolland later described you as the doctor of body and spirit who heals with medicine and melody.

What advice would you offer to individuals who want to make a positive impact on the world?

"Ah, the universal question! I was waiting for you to get to that one.

Here's what I know: Find something you are passionate about and serve others. Lead a life of honesty and empathy, and work for the greater good of mankind as much as you can.

Remember, you never know how even the smallest act of kindness can affect someone."

As day turns into night, the sounds of nature mingle with soft voices in the background of the tented area behind the hospital, surrounded by a thick forest.

Schweitzer rises and gazes thoughtfully over the restless river. When the silence has stretched for a moment, he looks up at me, and in his soft, introspective voice, says:

"Here in the forest, we are reminded that every life - human, animal, even the whispering trees - deserves reverence."

THE MUSE PERSPECTIVE

Schweitzer's unshakeable commitment to his patients during World War II demonstrated a moral courage that added a unique dimension to his legacy.

Once, the doctor trekked for miles to pick up a child suffering from malaria. When he returned, he was asked how he had managed to get the child over such unkind terrain.

"I did not carry him with my strength," Schweitzer replied, "but I carried him with my heart."

This unwavering commitment to humanitarianism inspired figures who saw in Schweitzer a personification of the best of humanity. Einstein declared, *"He is the only man of moral authority who can talk to the world."*

Schweitzer has also influenced the environmental movement, inspiring a greater awareness of our interconnection with the natural world and fostering a deeper value and respect for all living beings.

His musical scholarship and profound connection to Bach's music have influenced many composers, who have incorporated his philosophical ideas into their own works.

Many distinguished visual artists have created portraits and sculptures of Schweitzer. These convey his essence and uplift his message to the world: Love your neighbour as yourself, a reflection of love for all living beings.

Schweitzer's work in Africa resonated deeply with Du Bois, the American sociologist, socialist, historian, and Pan-Africanist civil rights activist.

He reminded the world that Schweitzer's dedication to serving the African people set a powerful example of interracial cooperation and rejecting racial prejudice.

He called "Schweitzer "the living conscience of Europe." As a Muse, Schweitzer inspired Du Bois to advocate for improved healthcare, education, and social justice for African Americans.

Even today, Schweitzer's message echoes through time - a call to live with reverence, compassion, and courageous service.

NOTE: For a highly readable and somewhat unusual biography, you may enjoy Albert Schweitzer: The Difficulty of Doing Good, Patricia Morris, Adam Rei Books, 2017

PABLO PICASSO

1881–1973

As a co-founder of the Cubist movement, Picasso pushed the boundaries of visual expression. His influence extends far beyond the confines of canvas and sculpture.

He was born in Málaga, Spain, and his genius was evident from an early age. However, the modernist titan took time to evolve.

His intense approach to art has made him an iconic figure in the cultural landscape and has impacted numerous areas of art and society.

PABLO PICASSO

Picasso was both the inspirer and the inspired. Today, I am meeting this most renowned artist in his later years.

This is a discreet private gallery in a serene space in the heart of Paris. It is also his studio on Rue des Grands-Augustins, where he would begin painting Guernica just days later.

This old Parisian townhouse has become a haven for contemporary artists and patrons.

As a Muse, Picasso has influenced countless figures from various disciplines: painters, writers, musicians, and film directors.

He has kindly agreed to discuss his impact as a Muse, his relationships with other creatives, and his role as a guiding force in their lives.

The architect of many visual art revolutions seems at ease in this quiet atmosphere, ideal for reflection and conversation.

As Picasso sits opposite me, I wonder aloud what he thinks about being a Muse to others and if he's OK with me calling him Pablo?

Picasso begins without further introductions. "Sure, Pablo will do. Anyway, you say you want to know about Muses?

Well, a Muse is not just the one who inspires, it's the one who ignites passion and fuels creation."

Thank you for that. Can you start with one of the most famous artists who found inspiration in your presence?

"Ah, I assume you mean Georges Braque. Yes, we jointly co-founded Cubism, but our relationship went far beyond mere collaboration.

Some would even say that while we interacted, there was no question of influence. I acted as a Muse to him regarding technique and spirit.

Georges had a hunger for newness, and our work together fed that. As we created it, Cubism was more than a form of art. It was a way of seeing the world differently, as if to say: Here is something new that has never been seen before."

Given your point about Braque, am I right that he was often seen as your shadow?

"I prefer the word companion. I offered him a deep well of inspiration that encouraged him to break away from traditional perspectives.

I wanted to encourage him to embrace a fragmented approach to the world.

Without our exchange of ideas and animated conversations, he would probably have stayed more grounded in the classical tradition. Whatever effect I had, Braque achieved a transformation that cemented his place in the avant-garde movement."

Beyond the art world, your influence has also reached the world of literature. How did that happen?

"You're talking, I suppose, particularly of Gertrude Stein, the American novelist and poet. She was inspired by my innovative approach to both form and subject.

Our friendship revolved around a creative interplay, with Stein's writing capturing the fragmented, multifaceted nature of my paintings. She also hosted marvellous dinners, where ideas flowed as freely as the wine.

It is gratifying to read how the innovative energy of my work stimulated her.

Together, we explored new frontiers in painting and literature, each influencing the other in an intellectually enriching and creatively fulfilling dynamic exchange."

You are being overly modest about your Muse effect. Stein said, *"I could never have written The Autobiography of Alice B. Toklas if not for Picasso."*

Picasso allows himself a smile of satisfaction: "It's true. She said I made her see the world through different eyes and gave her the freedom to write with a new voice and reject convention.

Our relationship was a turning point in her creative output. It allowed her to embrace a more abstract approach to writing, mirroring my visual approach to art."

Another figure who experienced the spark of inspiration from you was the Spanish filmmaker Luis Buñuel.

"Yes, Buñuel, we should talk about him. His work was already known for its surreal and often shocking qualities. I merely helped to accentuate its impact.

He gained from my ability to blend reality with abstraction, and I cherish his memorable comment:

"When I looked at Picasso's work, I understood that the line between the real and the imaginary was porous. That's when I knew how to approach cinema - not as a mirror of life, but as a playground for the mind."

Help me understand, Pablo. As a Muse, what did you do with him that affected this already talented creator so greatly?

"Buñuel was affected by my unrelenting drive to break from tradition. I showed him ways to challenge the viewer's perceptions and transform the ordinary into the extraordinary.

I explained that the artist is the one who sees. We are not bound by what is. We're the ones who can change how the world appears, how others experience it."

As a Muse, you also had a profound impact on other creatives. Would you like to discuss that briefly?

"I'd prefer others to do that. Let's merely say I was part of the avant-garde movements of the 20th century, including Dadaism, Surrealism, and Abstract Expressionism.

My yearning to invent style and subject matter affected artists and intellectuals who followed in my footsteps."

Can we explore the entire Muse role so that others can benefit from your experience? What do you need for inspiration to happen?

"The role of a Muse is like walking a tightrope. There's power in inspiring, yet there's a danger of losing yourself. I've seen it happen.

So, my advice? Never forget who you are, beyond the person you're inspiring. If you're the Muse, you must be more than the reflection they see in you.

Show them their limitations. Challenge their ideas, but never let their vision become your prison. If they want you to stay still, move. If they want you to be quiet, speak louder.

You must protect your creative fire. A true artist doesn't blot out the Muse or fail to listen. Instead, they fan their flame.

To be an active Muse is to keep the energy alive. Not merely by inspiring but by being unafraid to critique, collaborate, and challenge."

And what if they're afraid to respond to that?

"Walk away. It is better to burn brightly alone than to flicker out because of someone else.

With Braque, it was a dance. He might show me something, and I'd say, 'Good, but what *if this angle disappeared into the other, or could this be reversed and become something entirely new?*'

In such moments, I wasn't just offering ideas but inviting him into a shared space where creation was a dialogue, not a solitary act.

It was different with Dora Maar than with Braque. She was my subject of interest and my equal in passion, intellect, and artistry.

To act as her Muse, I had to respect the depths of her vision, which meant engaging with her as a creator, not merely as a passive observer or inspiration."

Although I know she was a French painter, photographer, and poet, how did she play a significant role in your life, personally and artistically?

"It's a good question since our relationship happened in the troubled periods of the Spanish Civil War and World War II.

Let me see, how can I sum it up simply for you? Dora became one of my most essential influences or Muses for a while.

I became obsessed with painting her since she had lovely dark hair, large eyes and an intense expression. I couldn't resist using her in my Weeping Woman series, where she symbolises grief and suffering.

She influenced my involvement, particularly my opposition to the Spanish Civil War.

In 1937, she helped me tackle my major work, Guernica. She documented the making of Guernica through photographs, providing invaluable historical insight into the process.

As a talented photographer, Dora brought a new perspective to my creative process, forming a two-way artistic relationship.

I cannot deny that Dora inspired some of my most profound and politically charged works during that period of my career.

Equally, I had a lasting influence on her and her contributions to art, particularly in photography and surrealism. I might sit beside her while she worked and ask, Why do you think light behaves differently when it touches a tear than when it touches a smile?

Or, when she was struggling with her photography, I'd say: *Break the frame, Dora. Don't let the lens tell you what's possible.*

Sometimes, I'd deliberately unsettle her - leave a drawing half-finished for her to critique or say: You only see shadows because you're afraid of what's in them."

Frankly, that sounds rather a cruel thing to say to her.

"This wasn't cruelty; it was my way of igniting something in her, pushing her to confront her fears and transform them into art.

Being her Muse meant stepping out of my ego to offer her a reflection of her power. I wanted her to recognise the endless potential within her pain, joy, and complexity. My aim was not just to inspire her.

I sought to provoke her to uncover things she never thought possible within herself."

This brings us to the complex issue of your relationships with women, how you interact with them, and the impact you have on them.

"I don't normally discuss such things, but if you want to raise something specific, go ahead."

Take, for example, Françoise Gilot, the accomplished artist and writer.

"Ah, yes - Françoise. What would you like to ask?"

You told her, "For me, there are only two kinds of women: goddesses and doormats."

Dora suffered a nervous breakdown following your relationship. Did you damage such women?

Pablo stares at me long and hard, a mixture of anger and grudging respect.

"You have certainly done your homework!

My relationships are woven into the fabric of my work. Love, or perhaps the absence of it, is central to my art. I've always been a man of extremes, and when I love, I give myself entirely, which often leads to chaos, disillusionment, and creativity.

But I, too, have had my Muses. For example, my first Muse, the French model and artist Fernande, carried me through the transition from the Blue Period into the Rose Period.

Her presence helped me rediscover joy and a kind of tenderness in my art. With her, the colour blue faded into the warm tones of pink, and I saw the world in a different light.

Love can make you see things as they are - or perhaps as they should be."

One productive result from her role as a Muse to you, Pablo, is that

you painted over 60 portraits of her. That's some Muse!

"But then came Olga, my first wife, a Russian ballerina. Olga was very different from anyone I had known before. I deeply admired her. She led me towards a more formal and classical approach to art, particularly in my depictions of her.

Our relationship was strained, driven by my ever-changing nature and my need for freedom. My work, especially the paintings in which I portrayed her, became a battleground.

It was all about passion and conflict, often reflected in the growing abstraction of my work. Then there's Jacqueline, my model, companion, confidante and second wife."

Since she has influenced your art, could you tell me how and when she came into your life?

"We met in 1952 at the Madoura Pottery Works in France, where Jacqueline was employed.

Despite a substantial age difference - she was 26, and I was 71 - our relationship blossomed.

More than any other woman who had inspired me, I couldn't stop creating her portraits.

She is also the most significant source of inspiration for my latest works.

I have long left the figurative world behind. Jacqueline is integral to this new phase of my life, and we have a peaceful relationship.

I think it's fair to say that I inspired her as an artist and a person. I've helped Jacqueline shape her identity and life's purpose.

As for inspiring others, I would say this: *My love life, personal storms, and the changes I underwent were just as integral to my story as any formal artistic lesson.*

Even those not directly involved in my struggles, such as young artists, understand that creativity isn't always about stability or calm. It's about the fire within, sometimes ignited by personal connections that might tear you apart.

My relationships have always reflected my artistic transformations. Love, jealousy, and heartbreak have continually made me explore new forms, discarding the old to create the new.

Each woman I loved and left behind expressed something I sought within myself. Admittedly, it was chaotic, but through it all, I learned to understand life's complexities more fully. And my art speaks to those complexities."

Thank you again for your time and for being so honest about the challenges and implications of being a Muse or having one yourself.

"For me, too, it has been a creative journey and a valuable reminder of some of the challenges I have faced."

THE MUSE PERSPECTIVE

Picasso produced an unbelievable amount of work, and it's hard to name and measure it.

His vast output helps explain why he's considered one of the most influential artists of the 20th century.

Picasso's most notable contribution was co-inventing Cubism, and his constant evolution through the Blue and Rose Periods marks his legacy on modern art.

Outside the canvas, Picasso's role as a Muse plays a key part in his legacy. His influence is evident in his ability to inspire other visual artists, writers, and filmmakers.

Through his collaborations, relationships, and examples, Picasso helped shape what art means today.

A living, breathing Muse whose fire still ignites the boldest minds of today.

NOTE: *If you wish to delve deeper into his life, there are numerous biographies and memoirs available.*

You may enjoy the in-depth Picasso: A Biography by Patrick O'Brian, W. W. Norton & Company, 1994.

VIRGINIA WOOLF

1882-1941

Virginia Woolf was a novelist who electrified literature, freeing it from tradition and infusing it with thought, sensation, and revolution.

To her, the medium was a story that could be told and a sensation to be experienced. She was not a bystander. Virginia was a provocateur who compelled the literary world to confront its exclusions and silences.

She did not seek adoration. Instead, this most insistent woman demanded change. Consequently, she made complacent fellow writers uncomfortable by demanding they think more incisively and daringly.

As a Muse, Virginia was never passive. Instead, she shaped literature or inspired those around her.

VIRGINIA WOOLF

I stand on the bank of the River Ouse in England - the afternoon light shimmers over the rippling water surface.

Virginia knows this quiet spot for our conversation very well. It is where she often walks, thinks, writes, and wrestles with the currents of her mind.

She is taller than I expected. Her delicate, angular frame seems to hang loosely inside her generously sized wool coat, which is both practical and elegant. Both of her hands plunge deeply into oversized pockets.

Her striking face is uniquely beautiful, captivating, and radiant. Her dark hair is loosely pinned back and slightly tousled. I perceive someone whose mind operates quickly.

I become acutely aware that this woman is observing me and the entire scene - the river, the sky, and perhaps even the shape of time itself.

This most potent Muse brushes my extended hand lightly as if granting touch on her own terms. Yet she offers a knowing smile of amusement and curiosity:

"You must forgive me; I am far more at ease with thoughts than gestures. But come, let us walk. The river listens well, and perhaps today, so shall we." She turns, inviting me to follow.

May I call you Virginia, or would you prefer something else? Perhaps 'Mrs. Woolf'? Or even 'Mrs. Leonard Woolf?

The corner of her mouth lifts with mild distaste: "Virginia will do. Anything else feels like a costume ill-fitted to the occasion.

Mrs. Woolf is what they print in reviews to remind the world that I am safely tethered to a husband. It's as if that makes my work more palatable.

And 'Mrs. Leonard Woolf - well, that belongs to another realm I hardly recognise as my own. So yes, Virginia will do."

Well, then, Virginia, let's start with why we're meeting today. How do you view your role as a Muse in the literary world?

"A Muse, you say? The world rarely bestows such a title upon a woman wielding a pen. Muses usually are meant to be seen, not heard. While they inspire, they never create.

Women Muses are assumed to be passive, sitting silently in the wings while men write, doing the great works that history deems worthy of recording.

A woman who writes is seldom content to exist as an object of inspiration. If anything, I am the one who stirs the water, who forces the imagination to work harder and think sharper."

So, you expect to provoke and disturb the surface of people's worlds?

"Yes, I make even the most self-confident minds second-guess their certainties. If I am a Muse, then call me a disruptive one. I'm a whisperer of unrest, a disruptor of peace.

I push against the boundaries of comfort and demand that those who dare to listen first see the world as it is and then as it might be.

Take E.M. Forster. He clung to tradition, was hesitant, and was wary of over-pushing his narratives. I challenged him to strip away the safety of Victorian sensibilities and embrace what was uncertain, fragmented, and ambiguous.

It wasn't easy for him. By refusing to let him rest in complacency, his work underwent a shift.

A Passage to India, for example, carries subtle yet present echoes of that challenge. Forster liked the idea of connection, of bridging divides.

'Look more deeply, I demanded. See that *no bridge is ever genuinely stable.*'

I did my best to raise his awareness of the implications for his writing. However, understanding another person is fraught, fragile, and riddled with failure.

Or consider Lytton Strachey, so sharp, clever and determined to dismantle the Victorian age with his irreverence.

Yet he only pretends to be the iconoclast. Certain conventions bind him, and he remains wary of exposing too much of himself.

While I admire his wit, I insist on yet more intimacy. His Eminent Victorians book may be his great act of rebellion, but I think I sharpened his blade. I reminded him that to tear down something correctly, one must understand every inch of its construction.

And then there's T.S. Eliot, so precise, so careful in his measured, modernist prose. He believes in control and mastery of form.

Well, I hungered for something wilder. When he read The Waste Land aloud to us in the rooms of the Omega Workshops, there was something raw there. Beneath all that most deliberate craft, I told him: *'You think you are containing chaos, but the truth is, it includes you.'*

I like to believe that thought lingered in his mind, unsettling him. It forced him to listen to the dissonance as much as the rhythm."

You apparently have no interest in being a Muse who watches and

reflects what others wish to see.

"That's correct. If I inspire, it is only by disruption, pushing where others hesitate. At precisely the moment one wishes for silence, I whisper What if?"

You also seem to feel that others impose the role of a Muse on you.

"Yes. Muses are often spoken of in longing tones as if they exist to be adored and captured.

I have never been a creature to be captured. I inspire because I challenge. With his steadfastness and belief in my mind, Leonard Woolf allows himself to be shaped by our discussions, debates, and shared convictions on literature as a revolutionary force.

I don't simply support his political ambitions; I demand more. I argue with him about the need for radical change.

The Hogarth Press we started together is not an indulgence. It's a revolution in print."

Virginia, may I ask you a rather intrusive question now? How do your struggles with mental health shape your creative influence?

"You may ask, and I will change your question to: What would my work be like without these struggles? Would I have seen Mrs. Dalloway's day unfolding in ripples of thought, one moment spilling into the next like waves upon a shore?

Would I have traced to the Lighthouse's ephemeral, shifting consciousness, with its ghosts of memory pressing against the present?

Would I have dared to write The Waves, where voices merge and dissolve, breaking against one another like the sea against the rocks?

I see the world as fragmented, impressionistic and drenched in feeling because my mind refuses the dullness of certainty. Madness, the world may call it.

But what is madness if not the mind straining against the limits imposed upon it? I have lived with its ebb and flow, the rising of dark tides, the moments of exquisite brilliance followed by unbearable silence.

I have known the terror of losing myself, of feeling the shape of my thoughts dissolve.

Yet, I have also touched a lucidity that few ever glimpse. I write while on the precipice and with the world shimmering with unbearable intensity."

And is your writing often responding to the seemingly inevitable constraints placed on women?

"Good question. We women have so little space to think. I write because the world does not want me to. My extended essay, A Room of One's Own, was not merely an argument but a weapon, a declaration of war. "

I drew attention to society's under-investment in women's education and the absence of women's voices telling their stories.

Women should claim financial and intellectual freedom to write. Instead, they ask us to be quiet, small, and Muse-like instead of creators."

Or, as you said at your Arts Society talk at Girton in 1928, a woman must have money and a room of her own if she is to write fiction.

"Exactly. Well, you have done your homework! Yes, it's not enough to complain about being excluded. "

I keep asking Why? What forces us from the pages, libraries, and desks where novels and essays are born? What weight of history, law, and silence makes their hands falter before they can write?

When I wrote A Room of One's Own, I was not just speaking of physical space, though that too is vital. I was referring to the mental, intellectual, and financial autonomy that women need to achieve.

How can they write when the world demands obedience, domestic servitude and silence?"

Tell me more about your relationship with Leonard Woolf. How does his influence affect your creative work?

"Leonard is the steadying force to my storm. He believes in my words when I don't. He presses the pages into print when my hands shake too much to hold them.

Be clear, though: Leonard is no jailer. He has never sought to contain me, only to ensure I do not shatter entirely. If my words reach the world, they walk on the bridge Leonard built.

Ours is not a marriage of convention or easy sentiment. We're bound not by duty but by something more profound - a shared belief in intellect, creation, and the necessity of thought.

Leonard stands watchful, unwavering, where others might dismiss my moments of darkness.

He does not recoil when the storms come, and my mind threatens to unmoor itself completely. He sits beside me. He carries me through.

He is not merely a caretaker coping with my fragility. Leonard is my first reader, fiercest critic, and most relentless champion. He neither flatters nor panders.

When I hand him pages that are still warm from my hands, he reads them with a mind honed like a scalpel, cutting where necessary and refining where needed.

He challenges me, sharpens me, and pushes me further than I might have dared to go alone.

My books exist not only because I wrote them but because Leonard creates the conditions in which they come alive.

He gave me the Hogarth Press, a gift far more than a printing press. It is freedom, a way to write without fear of rejection by the gatekeepers of the literary world.

Placing my words into his hands, I know they will not be at the mercy of those who might misunderstand or dilute them. They are ours, and he ensures they are set loose into the world, intact and unbowed."

Then there is Vita Sackville-West. What role does she play in shaping your creative process?

"Ah, Vita! After our first meeting at a rather disastrous dinner party in 1922, we got into the habit of exchanging flirty, lyrical letters. She is like firelight, flickering, elusive, and golden.

Vita lives in a world I did not know I might enter. It is filled with boldness and unapologetic pleasure. And, as the world now knows, I wrote Orlando for Vita."

You famously called it the longest love letter in literature!

"Thank you for that. Well remembered. Yes, Vita has made me playful and daring in new ways. My sentences are stretched, curved, and dance as never before."

So, in addition to being your lover, Vita is, by your description, also your Muse?

"Muse? There you go again! Certainly, Vita is not like the others. She doesn't tread carefully around me or treat me as delicate.

But Vita needs cautious handling. She strode into my life with the confidence of one who has never been told 'no.'

She lives as a man might, with freedom, adventure, and an unshakable certainty in her desires. Where I am cerebral and analytical, Vita acts. So yes, she makes me playful and daring."

That sounds to me, Virginia, like she is a Muse. Let's move on, though. What do you think about how modern feminists view your work?

"They read me, and I feel their eyes searching for echoes of their own struggle. That's the beauty of it.

The fight never ends. Each generation of women, thinkers, writers, and those who refuse to be silent takes up the work, shaping it anew.

I have no desire to be set in stone. Let me be air: shifting, necessary, impossible to contain.

I never mind being misunderstood; misreading is inevitable. History will always twist a writer to its own use, but I do fear being unread. To be unread is to be erased.

And what is a woman writer if not a voice battling against erasure? I have done my work when my words ignite something and are used as flares in the long dark struggle."

And for those who follow you, Virginia, what do you have to say to them?

"I tell them this: influence is not in grand gestures, proclamations or manifestos. It is in the quiet work of shaping thought. It is the courage to say what needs to be said.

My final message is: Do not ask if the world is ready for your voice. Instead, assume it is not and speak anyway."

THE MUSE PERSPECTIVE

Virginia Woolf was a Muse of fierce intelligence and deliberate rebellion. She did not passively inspire. Instead, she incited, provoked, and disturbed. Her work changed individuals and reshaped literature.

Her extended essay, A Room of One's Own, was a clarion call to women silenced by centuries of exclusion.

Virginia didn't just write novels; she transformed the novel form itself. Her stream-of-consciousness technique was no flashy stylistic device; it was a fundamental revolution in storytelling.

She did not do this alone; James Joyce also tried to capture consciousness in its raw form.

Virginia Woolf revolutionised the fiction landscape as we know it. History remembers Woolf as fragile and fierce, a paradox of strength and suffering. But her influence is inescapable.

She brought a new rhythm to literature, shook off gender conventions, and ensured that future generations of women wouldn't have to hunt for permission to write.

Virginia Woolf doesn't just survive. Like a subtle aroma, she continues to pervade literature.

NOTE: The world is awash with Woolf biographies. The most substantial is Hermione Lee's Virginia Woolf, Vintage, 1996.

Woolf's autobiographical writings are also powerful means of getting to know her.

Also, check out https://gutenberg.net.au/pages/woolf.html

IGOR STRAVINSKY

1882–1971

Igor Stravinsky revolutionised music. His groundbreaking compositions shaped the artistic destinies of Sergei Diaghilev, Vaslav Nijinsky, and Pablo Picasso.

He also significantly influenced Leonard Bernstein's conducting and composer Boulez's rigorous approach to music.

A fearless innovator, Stravinsky bridged classical and modern art, leaving an eternal legacy that inspires composers, choreographers, and artists worldwide."

IGOR STRAVINSKY

I am sitting in Stravinski's sunlit living room in his Hollywood home in 1949. It is late afternoon, and there's a faint hum of distant traffic.

The sixty-seven-year-old Igor Stravinsky is deeply immersed in his piano, focusing on the precise movements of someone deeply engaged in their craft.

The maestro adjusts his glasses. He straightens his back slightly, pressing the keys carefully but confidently.

He conveys the impression of a master who, though ageing, remains vigorous and alert.

After a few moments, with a barely perceptible, gentle resignation and as if reluctant to leave his creative space, Stravinsky comes and sits beside me.

Nearby, an animated and sharp-eyed friend, Robert Craft, sorts through scores and occasionally chimes in as our conversation begins. Stravinsky asks:

"Well, my curious friend, what exactly do you want of me today?"

Maestro, you've led a varied and exciting life, and you've had a profound impact on many. I am here to talk about your role as a Muse.

"A Muse. Well, yes, I have played that role from time to time."

Can we return to the beginning of your musical journey for a moment? What led you to become a full-time composer?

"Well, if you want to go that far back! I must first credit my family, who played a pivotal role in shaping my musical foundation.

"I was born in 1882 in Oranienbaum, Russia, into a family where music was integral to daily life. My father was a highly respected bass singer at the Mariinsky Theatre in St. Petersburg."

"Through him, I was exposed early to the power of operatic and classical music.

My mother, Anna Kholodovsky, was also musical, playing piano, though she remained a quieter influence."

"Despite this rich environment, it may be a surprise that my early education was not focused on a musical career."

"My parents, especially my mother, valued a traditional academic path and encouraged me to study law at St. Petersburg University."

"However, nature prevailed, and I was increasingly drawn to music, particularly during my association with the Rimsky-Korsakov family.

Nikolai, a giant of Russian composition and a close family friend, would become an essential guide and a lasting influence."

"Although I dabbled in music as a child, I didn't take it seriously until my late teens.

Rimsky-Korsakov's tutelage, which began around 1902, marked the formal beginning of my musical education.

He encouraged me to be highly disciplined in studying orchestration and introduced me to the craft of transforming musical ideas into attractive compositions.

My first big breakthrough into a professional music career came when Sergei Diaghilev, the impresario of the Ballets Russes, heard some of my early works.

Diaghilev saw promise in my orchestral pieces and invited me to compose for his revolutionary ballet company. This collaboration led to the creation of The Firebird in 1910.

Firebird proved to be a significant turning point for me and the Ballets Russes. Our joint success catapulted me onto the international stage almost overnight. Petrushka followed this in 1911 and, most famously, The Rite of Spring in 1913.

As I am sure you know, it shocked, inspired, and probably forever altered the landscape of classical music."

Was this rapid time of change and success the trigger for becoming a full-time composer?

"Not instantly. It was a process over time. My ballet's success and rising reputation as an audacious and innovative artist enabled me to devote myself solely to composition. But the journey wasn't always without bumps."

The shocks of World War I and the Russian Revolution, which shaped my attitudes and work style, led me to explore new forms and languages, including Neoclassicism.

Additionally, my parents and children provided tremendous moral support and creative input throughout this project.

The foundations I gained from childhood, the discipline of my law studies, and the influence of mentors like Rimsky-Korsakov all shaped me into a composer."

Pausing, he smiles, "Becoming a full-time composer was as much a matter of persistence and adaptability as it was of talent and opportunity.

I have profoundly loved this journey for all its twists and turns."

What is it like in Hollywood after those earlier years in Europe?

"Ah, Hollywood! It's not Paris, of course, or even Switzerland. But I've grown accustomed to it. Here, there's light and a kind of endless sun.

Here, too, I have space to think, although I confess that the American lifestyle requires an adjustment effort. But what matters is the work."

Speaking of which, I understand you've been collaborating with Robert Craft here.

"That's right; where are you, Robert?" From the corner comes a cheery: "Right here, Maestro."

Stravinsky gestures: "See, he's nearby and indispensable. We met only a short time ago. What was it, Robert, a year, perhaps two?

Yet, he is already like family. He understands my music, not just the notes, but the ideas behind them. Most importantly, he introduced me to ideas that challenged my intellectual curiosity.

It sounds like Mr. Craft has been something of a Muse to you rather than vice versa."

"A Muse? That word is too poetic. Robert is more like... an engine, a dynamo. He keeps me moving. He asks the hard questions.

He's very much a catalyst - a young mind whose questions compel me to refine my answers."

And what answers has he demanded from you, Maestro?

"Serialism, for one. I was always hesitant about Schoenberg and his twelve-tone methods. I thought they were too restrictive and mathematical.

But Robert here has shown me that there is room for freedom within these structures. He's pushed me to see this technique not as a cage but as a new language.

Craft adds almost in a whisper: "Maestro has always been a master of structure, of balance. Serialism is just another tool in his hands, like a brush to a painter."

Stravinski nods in agreement: "Precisely! And why should I not explore it? Am I not the same man who shocked Paris with The Rite of Spring? To challenge oneself is the only way to stay alive as an artist."

In the light of this latest phase of your work, Maestro, what drives your creative innovation?

"I discover the essence of music in contrasts: chaos and order, old forms with new life. My work communicates a shared instinct for rhythm and breath. It is primal yet structured."

Your collaborations with Sergei Diaghilev were legendary. How did you influence each other?

"Diaghilev was daring, like a conductor of visions. I gave him soundscapes that he exploded unexpectedly, further firing my imagination. What he gave me was sound and image.

Together, we reshaped ballet. The Firebird was the spark, but The Rite of Spring detonated with a force neither of us had predicted. It inspired Nijinsky's choreography, raw and revolutionary."

What about Pablo Picasso? How did a collaboration with him influence your work?

Picasso glimpsed what I hoped would be a reinterpretation of the tradition in Pulcinella. His brush evoked the spirit of my music. It highlighted the groundbreaking impact of the convergence of visual and musical modernism.

He translated my vision into designs that combined sound and image. In my opinion, that sort of symbiosis illustrates the potential of partnership."

You have motivated many people through your musical journey. How do you feel about serving as a Muse now?

"A Muse is not static but must irritate. For Diaghilev, I was the burning fire of music. For Nijinsky, the dancer and choreographer, it was the rhythmic force he had to resist, interpret, or break free from."

For Picasso, it was a rebellion against tradition. My plea to people like Bernstein and Boulez is to think anew.

Let me put it this way. My work encourages artists to go beyond limits."

Stravinsky returns to the piano and plays a few contemplative chords, then resumes his seat, relaxed yet intensely engaged in our discussion of people influenced by his work.

What about others, like Leonard Bernstein or Pierre Boulez? Do you see yourself as an influence, even a Muse, to them?

"I suppose, in a sense, yes. But a Muse is not always a figure who inspires beauty and harmony.

Sometimes, a Muse provokes, challenges, and unsettles. I believe that is what I represent to Bernstein and Boulez."

Yet another pause, and this time he again looks at me intensely: "Lenny - ah, young Bernstein! What an extraordinary talent! He is, how do you say it, larger than life? He has boundless energy and a theatricality that is almost contagious.

He conducts my work as though he is channelling not just me but something universal. Even if you know the music, he makes it sound like you are listening to it for the first time.

When interpreting The Rite of Spring or Petrushka, he doesn't just follow the score; he brings it alive with his vitality.

It is as though my music becomes a springboard for his ideas. He always adds something of himself, but in doing so, he keeps the music alive and relevant.

Perhaps he does see me as a Muse, but I see his interpretations as proof that my work can transcend time and place.

Bernstein seems to find in my music the freedom to be bold. Maybe I should remind him that music can be rigorous and wildly expressive.

If I inspire him, it's by showing that these two things are not opposites but complementary.

I particularly appreciated his interpretations of my work, which he described so well in his lecture series."

And Pierre Boulez?

"Such a very different spirit. Where Bernstein approaches music with fire, Boulez is all ice, pure, sharp, precise.

For instance, when conducting The Rite of Spring, Boulez approaches it not as a primitive outburst but as an exquisitely structured masterpiece.

Boulez is a revolutionary who, to me, appears to be someone who dares to upend tradition. To Boulez, I am a Muse not for what I have done but for what I represent.

He has even called me a great architect, and perhaps he is right. But what Boulez finds in me is not just structure; it is the idea that art must evolve and break from the past to create something new.

For him, I am the artist who refuses to stand still. His fascination with my work is intellectual, almost mathematical in nature.

He dissects my scores and finds the logic beneath the surface. In doing so, he builds upon my legacy, pushing music further into the modern age."

It seems, Maestro, that you serve as a kind of guiding force for Bernstein and Boulez, though in very different ways.

"Yes, and this is as it should be. Art is not meant to be static. If my work inspires them to take different paths - Bernstein toward the emotional and theatrical, Boulez toward the intellectual and abstract-then I am doing my job as a composer.

It is strange to speak of Muses, especially at my age. To be a Muse is not to dictate; it is to provoke, to open doors that others might walk through."

With that, Stravinsky ends our conversation in a way that feels most comfortable to him.

Without any goodbye, he returns to his piano and begins to play. Robert Craft and I are transfixed, sharing a look of admiration for this most amazing Muse.

THE MUSE PERSPECTIVE

Igor Stravinsky remains one of the most revolutionary and influential composers in music history.

His life traversed a century of artistic transformation, marked by constant evolution as Stravinsky strove to reinvent himself throughout his career.

Stravinsky became exposed to diverse and, for him, new artistic movements. His later explorations of moving away from formal musical structures and into serialism were influenced by colleagues such as Robert Craft.

This readiness to consider new ideas helped Stravinsky remain interesting to subsequent generations of musicians.

With increasing age, Stravinsky's role as a Muse became more apparent. Stravinsky's ability to elicit diverse responses from two towering figures, such as Bernstein and Boulez, underscores the breadth of his influence.

Craft and others found in Stravinsky a model of never-ending creativity and adaptability.

Through his music, Stravinsky showed how an artist could remain vital, relevant, and daring well into old age.

His role as a Muse was dynamic and multidimensional, rooted in his relentless drive to reinvent himself and challenge tradition.

His music continues to inspire across emotional and intellectual boundaries. Stravinsky saw himself as a provocateur, an artist who compelled others to enter new creative territories.

His legacy endures in his compositions and the generations of creators who continue to find their creative spark in him.

NOTE: You may also enjoy Michael Oliver's Stravinsky (Phaidon, 2008).

ELEANOR ROOSEVELT

1884–1962

In a fictional line from a TV series, President Franklin Roosevelt offered a jocular apology to a recently arrived White House guest:

"I'm sorry my wife, Eleanor, is not here, as she's off somewhere running the country." The quip captured the essence of the First Lady of the United States.

Eleanor Roosevelt was a significant muse of great influence. She defied the expectations that the First Lady held a mere backroom role.

Through compassion, courage, and relentless advocacy for equity and human dignity, Eleanor demonstrated that a Muse can also be an activist.

It is no wonder, then, that Eleanor was consistently voted one of the most admired women in America for many years.

ELEANOR ROOSEVELT

Franklin Roosevelt died in 1945, and now it's 1950. I am meeting Eleanor in her study at Val-Kill, Hyde Park, New York.

This is her retreat and workspace, distinct from the grandeur of the Roosevelt family estate, Springwood. This space is modest yet undeniably elegant, a true reflection of its owner.

The bookshelves brim with well-worn volumes, and the desk is scattered with letters, confirming this is a woman of intellect and action.

Tall windows look out onto the tranquil beauty of the Hyde Park countryside. Sunlight brightens the bookshelves, which are filled with works on politics, philosophy, and social reform.

Seeing this most distinguished Muse sitting in an armchair, her hands resting on a letter she has just finished drafting, allows me to study the woman I will soon be talking to.

In her late sixties, Eleanor radiates strength, warmth, and intelligence. Her kind, expressive face features soft contours and large eyes, conveying a sense of empathy and attentiveness.

Her prominent nose is well-shaped, and with a slightly square jawline, her face conveys a firm yet gentle impression. She is dressed in an elegant outfit accented by a brooch and a string of pearls. She turns to me with a friendly smile.

"Welcome. I believe you're particularly interested in a subject dear to my heart: how to exercise influence to promote cherished causes. Where would you like to start?"

Mrs Roosevelt, I want to ...

"Just call me Eleanor; it'll be much simpler!"

Yes, of course. Eleanor. Your public service is extensive, and you accomplish a great deal. Where did this busy, highly organised person come from?

"Well, I was once a fearful, anxious conformist, a person who wouldn't say boo to a goose."

Weren't you once something of a doormat, while today you're more like a dynamo?

Eleanor giggles, enjoying the imagery: "From doormat to dynamo! I love it.

What you describe is true. When I was young, I was very self-conscious. Little by little, as life unfolded, I faced each problem as it arose.

It wasn't until my thirties that I began to find myself and understand the power of compassion. I discovered how to resist pointless conformity and press for change.

As my activities and work expanded, I never tried to shirk responsibility. I have always tried to avoid evading an issue. When I found something to do, I just did it."

Could you please help me understand how that happened, Eleanor?

"When I first got married, I was often pregnant and worried about my six children. One of whom did not survive.

As you can imagine, they also required a significant time investment. My husband's political career and a large family didn't leave much room for me.

Gradually, though, I realised that prominent advocacy work would play a significant role in my life, and I learned a great deal about the challenges of family life, especially for women.

I grew increasingly empathetic toward women's rights and family-oriented policies.

Juggling my children's needs with public life gave me direct insight into the trials of women balancing family and career.

Then, I had seven difficult years helping Franklin recover from his attack of polio.

It's not surprising that people hardly saw much of me; in today's media terms, I had an almost invisible public persona."

Yet today, you have become a Muse to the nation with outspoken views and a reputation for challenging the status quo.

"Muse to the nation! I love your metaphors. But really, all I've done is show people that they've a better side and that change is possible, even if it takes time.

I discovered the joy of giving, and it was liberating. I stopped being a colourless echo. Instead, I began to enjoy suggesting new standards of public life and challenging overprotective rules."

For example, when the aviator Amelia Earhart came to town, we took a ride in her plane for a midnight spin, evading the security team's constraints.

With my journalist friend, Hick, I gradually improved my ability to handle the media. For example, instead of holding the traditional all-male press conferences, I began hosting my own all-women's conferences.

I know some critics say I try to do too much for people. But my golden rule is whatever comes your way, you have to handle it."

There are so many causes for you to support. Can you explain how you balance the demands on your attention?

"Balance is a curious word; it's more like weaving threads into a fabric. These threads are interconnected, whether advocating for civil rights, supporting the war effort, or championing workers' rights.

If there's a single link for dealing with them, it's staying true to my principles while being open to growth and learning."

One of your most recognised principles is your strong belief in civil rights. How did you tackle these vicious trends in our society?

"With persistence. I have relentlessly used my daily media column, My Day, to condemn current behaviour trends and make frequent speeches arguing for America to show the world its better side.

When my husband, Franklin, was the US President, I constantly pressed him to introduce legislation to ban segregation and to make lynchings illegal, with accompanying law enforcement.

Unfortunately, Franklin resisted then, not because he agreed with such practices but because he said he needed to keep the Southern Democrats on his side.

So, I changed my strategy to pursue the remedies. I have been going to the people, raising pressure through increased public awareness. In that way, the citizens, not the politicians, demand change."

Where do you find the courage to challenge the status quo on segregation and prejudice, especially in such a polarised society?

"It's a good question, but you don't need to be fearless to act against the status quo. What's more important is to recognise the urgency of the moment.

I often recall the 1939 incident with Marian Anderson, the magnificent contralto.

The Daughters of the American Revolution, an organisation I belonged to, refused to let her perform in Constitution Hall due to her race.

I resigned from the organisation, which led to an even more historic concert at the Lincoln Memorial. Remaining silent would have made me complicit in injustice."

Marian Anderson credits you with acting as a Muse, giving her a platform that changed her career.

Did you realise, at the time, the ripple effect your support might create?"

"No, since I didn't do it for recognition. I acted because it was the right thing to do.

Seeing how Marian's voice moved people, broke barriers, and inspired generations strengthened my conviction that we must help one another.

Marian's success showed that talent and humanity can transcend the limits others impose.

An earlier factor in my ability to challenge the status quo was my attendance at Allenswood Academy in London, where I was mentored by the progressive educator Marie Souvestre.

She became a key influence on my intellectual and emotional development. Souvestre encouraged me to read widely, think critically, and engage in social and political issues.

I gained a passion for learning and social justice from her that has never left me. Souvestre's teachings were based on liberal, humanistic values.

She was ahead of her time in advocating for gender equality, social justice, and global citizenship. Highly practical, she founded schools that welcomed students from various backgrounds.

Her schools fostered an environment that encouraged young women to discuss politics, literature, and philosophy.

That's a most helpful picture of influences on your development. Are there other such individuals or influences you would like to discuss?

"I had an eye-opening experience as an active volunteer with the American Red Cross during the First World War.

I visited numerous hospitals and didn't just take a grand tour. Instead, I spent hours speaking with wounded soldiers, writing letters on their behalf, and offering comfort.

Some of them asked me to make contact with their parents to say they were alive and in rehab. I made sure all these requests were followed through.

I was directly exposed to human suffering, which had a profound and lasting impact on me.

I discovered the importance of a hands-on approach when distributing supplies and assisting in hospital activities. The emotional toll strengthened my desire to help others and improve their conditions.

It taught me invaluable lessons in empathy, resilience, and the power of direct action."

You mentored future leaders, such as John F. Kennedy. How did

this support affect his career?

"When I first met Kennedy, I didn't rate his vision highly; it needed much more focus. So, I urged him to go beyond his immediate ambitions and consider the broader implications of his decisions.

Later, he credited our discussions with shaping his civil rights stance and commitment to public service."

You had considerable influence on Frances Perkins and had tangible success in your role as a Muse.

"Yes, she became the first woman to reach the U.S. Secretary of Labor position. We shared a strong joint belief in the dignity of workers, and Frances wanted to establish Social Security and provide protections.

I supported her because I knew these would transform people's lives. Her determination complemented my advocacy, and we jointly pushed boundaries to create lasting change. She was a trailblazer."

Your work during the Great Depression and, more recently, in the war effort has been outstanding. How have you maintained hope during such challenging times?

"It's entirely wrong to view hope as a luxury. I think it is a necessity.

Seeing people's hardships, listening to their stories and advocating for programs to ease their suffering convinced me that hope stems from witnessing their strength and doing everything I could to support them."

Many see you as a source of inspiration, a Muse, and others as a model change agent. How do you view those two roles?

"I see myself as a catalyst, not a Muse in the classical sense. I fulfil my purpose if my actions motivate others to pursue justice and equality.

The world needs dreamers and doers alike, and I strive to bridge the gap between the two."

Your weekly media column, My Day, continues to reach millions of Americans. It must take a great deal of work. What impact do you hope to achieve?

"Yes, My Day demands careful organisation, but I have help. It is my way of connecting with people directly and sharing my experiences, thoughts, and reflections.

I want readers to see me as a friend and mentor. I'm determined to inspire my readers with unwavering optimism and a sense of duty.

I write almost every weekday, covering a range of topics, including politics, social issues, human rights, and sharing my observations and experiences.

It is gratifying to know that my column is said to be one of the most widely read and influential.

Even in a position of influence, you must remain human, striving to make sense of and improve the world."

I've achieved my goal if my words encourage others to act or think. This sense of empowerment makes people feel they have a role in shaping society.

Sharing daily thoughts and activities inspires readers with a sense of duty. I mainly want to reassure people that their struggles are understood and that progress, however slow, is possible."

You've filled so many roles while staying deeply grounded. Eleanor. Could you share what sustains your drive and compassion?

"There's nothing complicated about what you've asked, since

sustaining a drive can test even the strongest resolve. Persistence and drive are rooted in resilience, which I learned as a child.

Early on, marriage to Franklin revealed the power of partnership to bolster resolve, even in the face of adversity.

Most of all, though, I am sustained by the letters I receive from people around the world. Their stories of courage remind me that our collective strength lies in three essentials: empathy, solidarity and compassion.”

I wonder if you could suggest one person or an action you are most proud to have had a direct impact on.

“It’s kind of you to put it that way. I’m particularly proud of my connection with Mary McLeod Bethune, the distinguished African-American educator and civil rights leader.

We developed a close friendship, which ultimately led to her becoming the first African American woman to head a federal agency.

I’m also incredibly proud of my role in helping to launch the Universal Declaration of Human Rights in 1948.

As the Chair of the United Nations Commission on Human Rights, I was involved with its drafting, advocating, and ultimately gaining consensus for the declaration.”

You’ve been tireless in advocating its principles.

“Yes, I have travelled widely in support of the Declaration. I do my best to promote human rights and inspire governments, non-profits, and individuals to incorporate the Declaration’s ideals into their policies and lives.”

Finally, Eleanor, do you ever think about what legacy you’ll leave behind?

"My greatest wish is that those who come after me will continue to build a world where every individual has the opportunity to thrive."

THE MUSE PERSPECTIVE

During her years as First Lady, Eleanor Roosevelt aroused admiration and, simultaneously, a torrent of vituperation.

While amassing numerous devotees, her behaviour towards those she enraged raised questions of power: gaining access to it and the semblance of control.

However, Eleanor's power as a Muse did not derive from her role as the president's spouse. It grew out of her admirable ability to sense motivators in people.

Her Tomorrow is Now, published posthumously, called on future generations to engage in civic life and social justice.

President Kennedy's speeches and policies frequently invoked Eleanor's commitment to moral responsibility and public service.

Former President Bill Clinton said, alluding to the famous Kennedy "We Choose to Go to the Moon" speech, that it embodied the moral urgency and drive inherent in Eleanor herself.

Kennedy's relationship with his Muse, Eleanor, almost certainly helped launch the US Peace Corps. The Corps modelled her ideals of international cooperation and grassroots action.

Her influence was evident in Kennedy's eventual embrace of civil rights, including his 1963 call for expansive legislation - a moment that many historians acknowledge as a turning point for the movement.

As chair of the United Nations Commission on Human Rights, she directed the efforts to produce the Declaration of Human Rights in 1948.

It remains one of the most significant global achievements of the 20th century. It laid the foundation for modern human rights law and influenced worldwide treaties, conventions, and national constitutions.

Eleanor Roosevelt was not one to limit herself to advice-giving. In her 50s, she delivered more than 150 speeches a year. She helped mould a generation of leaders who would carry on her legacy.

As a quite literally tireless advocate and influencer, Eleanor proved that courage, compassion, and action have the power to change societies.

Franklin has the final say. As he once said, with mock exasperation: 'Jesus, just let Eleanor be tired.'

NOTE: For more about this marvellous Muse, don't miss the succinct and well-written Eleanor Roosevelt's Life of Searching and Self-discovery by Ann Atkins, Flash History Press.

You may also like The Autobiography of Eleanor Roosevelt, published by Bloomsbury Academic in 2022.

GEORGIA O'KEEFFE

1887–1986

She is one of the most recognisable names in American modernism. Georgia O'Keeffe is renowned for her innovative and powerful flower paintings, New Mexico landscapes, and reduced forms that have made her work iconic.

O'Keeffe's independence, artistic vision, and profound connection to nature inspired innumerable artists, writers and cultural figures.

Her life and work are icons of creative freedom and the enduring strength of the individual in art. She was incredibly famous at a time when art was overwhelmingly defined and dominated by men.

GEORGIA O'KEEFFE

I'm in Abiquiú, New Mexico, in the early 1950s, and sitting with artist and Muse Georgia O'Keeffe.

The warm afternoon light fills this small room, and there's just a faint, soft rustling of the wind moving through the tall grass outside.

Her artwork fills the walls with large, bold flowers, distant desert landscapes, and evocative animal bones. The conversation is intimate and, for me, a little unexpected.

You are most kind, Georgia, to agree to meet and discuss what it means to be a Muse.

"Do you know," she begins, her voice low and deliberate, "that I wanted to avoid being anyone's Muse for ages? It felt like such a passive role, to inspire someone else's work but not have the power to make it your own.

When I was younger, I felt that the word 'Muse' almost turned the person it was meant to describe into just an object.

Gradually, though, I have realised the role of a Muse is not always so one-dimensional.

Being a Muse can be empowering, and the energy you give to the artist - your form, presence, and spirit-can be a gift or an invitation to see the world differently.

I have found that what's important is never losing yourself in someone else's vision.

In a way, it must be mutual. Yes, you give, but you also receive something in return. And what you offer is ultimately transformed, in one way or another."

You've long been considered a Muse to many, especially your husband, the photographer Alfred Stieglitz.

"Alfred… well, Alfred was unlike anyone I'd ever met. Frankly, at first, I wasn't sure about him. This was a powerful man with a mind able to see through you and extract things about you that you didn't even know were there.

He seemed to see something in me before I saw it myself, and it wasn't only about my physical appearance.

He adored photographing me. During the 1920s and 1930s, Stieglitz produced over 300 portraits of me. And I admit some of them captured me in ways I couldn't have imagined.

Those photographs established you as a modernist icon, and he was the first to exhibit your work in 1916. How did that dynamic shape you as an artist?

"He saw my inner world and detected my potential as an artist.

At first, I resisted his impact and insights because I wanted to be my own artist, independent and free from the expectations of being anyone's Muse.

But Alfred… pushed me, not overtly, but in how he spoke about my work and how I saw the world.

He recognised something in me that I had trouble acknowledging. It's hard to explain, but he helped me take that next step, helped me trust in my vision."

You were the Muse but also a creator in your own right.

"Yes, especially in the early years, there was always a certain tension. People would see me as a figure in his work, and they would say things like,

Oh, you're the woman in his photographs, or you're the inspiration for his art.

And I understood that our connection was undeniable. People saw me as his Muse, yet I wasn't always sure how to feel.

Eventually, I found my path over time and began to see my work as just as important, if not more so."

When did you start seeing your art as more than just a reflection of someone else's vision?

"A good question! I admit that it wasn't an easy realisation. I was constantly questioning myself, always wondering if I was riding on the coattails of someone else's reputation.

Then, one day, after several trips there, I decided to leave New York and move to New Mexico.

I thought, 'If I'm going to be serious about this, if I am going to be my own artist, I must create in my own space. I needed the solitude, the space to breathe, to think.

And that's when I truly began finding my voice. The landscapes, the desert, the mountains all spoke to me in a way I hadn't expected.

In 1945, I bought this house in Abiquiú, New Mexico and now spend some time restoring it.

Her face brightens as she recalls the moment: "I think it was the freedom of being alone with my thoughts that allowed me to see things clearly, to understand what I wanted to say.

And it wasn't just about the subjects, the flowers, the bones, the landscapes. It was about how they affected me, how I perceived them, and how I could genuinely convey them.

That's when I began trusting myself fully as an artist. But even then, I had to work hard to silence the doubt.

It was always there, lurking, a voice that said, 'Who are you to claim the title of an artist? But I realised that doubt was just part of the process and something I had to live with."

You've often said, "I don't want to be defined by any one thing." **Do you still feel that way?**

"Yes. Even now, I resist being pinned down by labels. People often want to classify things to make them easy to understand and sell.

However, my work… well, cannot be easily categorised. That's why I resisted being just a 'flower painter' for so long.

I painted flowers, true, but I painted them in a way that felt more symbolic and deeply connected to my world. They weren't just pretty images but expressions of life, of the world's vastness and fragility.

And that's how I want my work to be seen, not just as a product of a moment, but as a reflection of something more enduring.

Your work has had a profoundly impactful effect on the way people perceive the natural world. What is it about your art that has resonated with so many people?

I believe it's how I perceive things. It's interpreting and translating them into something that resonates with people more deeply.

I had to create on the canvas an equivalent of what I felt about what I was observing, rather than merely replicating it.

When I paint a flower, I'm not just showing you what it looks like, but what it feels like and represents.

That's why I painted flowers so large - they weren't just small objects anymore; they were grand, monumental. They simultaneously became symbols of strength, beauty, fragility, and the essence of life.

And I think people respond to that, and something universal in my work. It's not just reflecting the desert, flowers, or bones; it's about life in all its complexity.

I strive to capture something timeless that resonates with the essence of who we are. My life has no easy answers or simple categories. It's a struggle to grow and retain a fierce independence."

Your life here in New Mexico appears to be deeply fulfilling. Did you ever wish for a family or children?

"No, Alfred and I grew apart, and his infidelity made things hard for me to bear. When he died, I became even more attached to Mexico and decided to devote my life to my art.

Anyway, motherhood would have conflicted with my painting."

You've already lived such a vibrant life, Georgia. What do you hope people take away from your work? What do you want your legacy to be?

"I want people to understand that art is not just about what you see. It's about what you feel, what you know in your heart.

I hope my work will remind people to see the beauty in the world around them, to appreciate it, and to respect it. I also hope it will inspire others to trust their voices and to create from that deep place of knowing within themselves.

That's what I've always wanted: to inspire people to see the world in a new way, to allow them to look at every day with fresh eyes."

After meeting with this Astonishing Muse and stepping out into the soft New Mexico sunlight, I feel I've glimpsed something extraordinary in this person of quiet strength.

She's a Muse who has shaped art history through her vision and found her voice through unyielding determination.

THE MUSE PERSPECTIVE

Georgia O'Keeffe attracted international recognition for her meticulous paintings of natural forms, particularly flowers and desert-inspired landscapes.

These paintings often depict places where she lived and made such an impact that she became known as the Mother of American Modernism.

O'Keeffe's profound influence rippled outwards, far beyond her husband, Alfred Stieglitz.

For example, she inspired the photographer Edward Weston, who often drew parallels between her artistic explorations of nature and his own.

Ansel Adams, famed for his American landscape photographs, was deeply moved by O'Keeffe's interpretations of the Southwest.

He was especially taken with the interplay on her canvases between vast landscapes and intimate natural details.

Many female painters have been influenced by how O'Keeffe balanced modernism with personal expression.

Writers inspired by O'Keeffe include D.H. Lawrence, with whom she has corresponded and visited his ranch in New Mexico.

Lawrence admired her as an artist and found inspiration in her focus on primal, natural forms. His literary explorations of nature and vitality often align with themes in O'Keeffe's works.

Contemporary musicians and performers have drawn inspiration from O'Keeffe's life as a Muse for their work.

For example, Patti Smith, the American singer, songwriter, poet, painter, author, and photographer, has spoken of O'Keeffe's life and landscapes as "symbolic of creative authenticity."

O'Keeffe-inspired filmmakers, too. For instance, filmmaker Martin Scorsese admired O'Keeffe's ability to capture the essence of America through her art.

He remarked that just as cinema aims to transcend the screen, O'Keeffe's paintings evoke a sense of place and emotion that transcends the canvas.

Renowned film director David Lynch also drew inspiration from O'Keeffe's work, particularly her exploration of natural forms and landscapes.

He explained that the abstraction in O'Keeffe's work opens up a world of possibilities, allowing the viewer to experience the familiar in an entirely new way.

In addition to being a muse for individuals, O'Keeffe was a Muse for movements and ideas.

Her retreat to New Mexico and the life she created there took on the aura of artistic freedom, which involved being always in harmony with the land.

Fashion designers such as Donna Karan and Calvin Klein have noted O'Keeffe's minimalist clothing and aesthetics as an inspiration for contemporary fashion.

Her aesthetic, which emphasised simplicity and natural beauty, had a Muse-like impact on the creative industries.

O'Keeffe engaged with multiple disciplines and generations. She personified a blend of modernist thought and cultural independence.

Her influence as a muse extended beyond how others perceived her; it also shaped how her life and work inspired new ways of thinking and creating.

NOTE: There are two O'Keeffe Museums: one in Santa Fe and the other in Abiquiú, New Mexico, 52 miles away.

htt3ps://www.okeeffeMuseum.org/about-georgia-okeeffe/

You may also enjoy Randall Griffin's beautifully illustrated and informative commentary on this marvellous Muse: Georgia O'Keeffe, Phaidon Focus 2014.

GALA DALÍ

1894-1982

Gala Dalí was unstoppable. Her energy was a catalyst for change. She transformed the traditional role of the artist's wife into that of a strategist, a commanding presence, and a muse who actively shaped the legacies of those around her.

Gala was born in Russia, and early in life, she hurled herself into the centre of Surrealism in Paris. This Muse delivered masterclasses in ambition and reinvention, from inspiring the poet Paul Éluard to orchestrating Salvador Dalí's ascent to surrealist legend.

GALA DALÍ

In the sun-dappled garden of Dalí's house in Portlligat, Spain, there's a tang of sea salt and a faint rustle of olive trees.

Shadows stretch lazily on the whitewashed walls, playing their part in Dalí's surrealist world.

Amid this dreamy tableau, Gala sits majestically on a throne-like yellow couch. She is as arresting as the objects around her: a lopsided clock, enormous crimson lips, and a giant lobster that seems to challenge reality.

She has agreed to meet to discuss the role of Muse. Now that I'm here, Gala Dalí stares boldly at me, as if she knows exactly what I'm thinking.

"Call me Gala," she offers unasked, as if bestowing a great gift. Then she picks up her delicate porcelain cup of tea from a low table, the handle shaped like a swan's neck and takes a dainty sip.

"Everyone asks what it means to be a muse," she begins. "They expect some secret formula, a divine gift. But they miss the point entirely.

To be a muse is both to receive inspiration and to command it. I did not wait for the world to define me; I changed myself into the muse I chose to become."

Could you tell me more about your early life, Gala?

With the precision of someone who has told this story many times and always on her terms, she tilts her head, considering the question.

"My childhood was… well, unremarkable, I suppose. A good Russian girl was sent to Switzerland to recover from tuberculosis.

But even in the stillness of the sanatorium, I learned something important: Life does not pause for those who hesitate. I saw it in the girls who would weep over letters from their families, expecting someone else to decide their future.

I swore to myself that I would never wait.

I had two older brothers, Vadim and Nicolai, and a younger sister, Lidia. I spent my childhood in Moscow, and my father died when I was eleven years old.

Mother remarried later to a lawyer. I related well to her and acquired a good education thanks to her.”

Were you a good student or rebellious even then?

“I graduated with a very high average grade from the academy for young ladies. It gave me the power to be a primary school teacher and to teach people in their own homes.

When I was eighteen, my tuberculosis grew worse, and my family placed me in a Swiss sanatorium. That is where I met my future husband, Paul Éluard. We became good friends because we were about the same age and shared a love of reading.

We were both released from the sanatorium in 1914. I returned to Russia, Éluard, to the war front, but we got engaged first. We married in 1917, and my only daughter, Cécile, was born the following year.

Books had been my sanctuary. In their pages, I escaped the crushing monotony of my early life in Russia. When my mother died, I felt untethered and abandoned.

And then came my stepmother - a woman who felt more like a stranger than family.

Those years forged my independence but left scars I carry today."

So, when did you discover the emerging avant-garde movement?

"In my early twenties, when Éluard and I lived in Paris. It was the epicentre of cultural and artistic evolution, brimming with the work of artists, writers, and philosophers.

They were questioning the very nature of reality, as well as the hidden depths of the newly emerging concept of the psyche.

As a poet, Éluard formed close relationships with the leading figures of the Surrealist movement, particularly with the creators of the literature magazine founded by Breton and others.

I attended some of their meetings and met Max Ernst. Max painted me in several of his portraits, and I also became friends with the poet René Émile Char.

Surrealism was deeply committed to unlocking human desires and dreams. Its magnetic pull drew me in. This was no mere artistic rebellion but a revolution exposing raw, unfiltered human desires.

For someone like me, with a past marked by repression and yearning, surrealism was more than art; it was a liberation.

It allowed me to explore the depths of my mind and emotions without apologising."

When did you first meet Salvador?

It's a long saga. When Dalí went to Paris to present the film he'd created with Luis Buñuel, Un Chien Andalou. In 1929, the Belgian poet and gallery owner Camille Goemans introduced Dalí to my husband, Paul Éluard.

Dalí invited him and several others to spend the summer in Cadaqués, Catalonia, Spain. That's how I met Dalí and spent time there with my daughter, Cécile.

For Dalí, meeting me was love at first sight. In his book, Secret Life, he wrote that I was destined to become his heroine, who would bring psychological healing to the main character.

From that time onward, my fate was with Salvador."

Did you ever feel conflicted about leaving Éluard when you met Dalí?

"Conflicted? No! Paul and I had become echoes of what we once were. Love must evolve, or it withers.

I wasn't leaving Paul when I met Dalí; I was stepping into something new. Dalí was chaos incarnate, brilliance waiting to be harnessed.

I saw a genius who needed grounding, and I knew I could be the force to shape his destiny.

In 1958, Dalí and I married in a chapel near Girona, and a decade later, he bought me the castle in Pubol, Spain."

Is this the famous lover's retreat?

With a sudden intake of breath, Gala snaps back at me: "None of your business." Then, thinking better of it, she offers a knowing smile as she tilts her head thoughtfully:

"Do you know what Tarot card kept turning up when I cast the horoscope for today's conversation with you?"

With a dramatic flourish with her hand, she announces: "The Page of Cups!" She giggles softly as though sharing a delightful secret.

"A curious little dreamer, always peeking into that strange cup of his, expecting to find fish, stars, or maybe even a reflection that doesn't belong to him.

He's like a child trying to catch bubbles with a net… or perhaps like us, wondering what odd shapes our words will take when they land between us.

Could that be you, by any chance?" She pauses and then gives a little laugh.

"Yes, all right, what else was I supposed to do, a sexy woman on the loose? Dalí could give me much, but was incapable of sexual love.

He preferred masturbation, and I couldn't put up with that, so the castle became my refuge."

Can I ask about how Dalí's friends saw you? Many of them disapproved of you, didn't they?

Gala again inhales deeply. Standing, she fixes me with her baleful eyes as if wanting the earth to swallow me. Then she stalks off, leaving me regretting my temerity in raising the issue.

Just as quickly, she returns and sits down beside me.

"Always peeking into that strange cup of yours, eh? Those fellows didn't understand; that's why they hated me. One of them even called me a parasite.

When I met Dalí, he was like a child, terrified and insecure. Few of his pictures sold, and he was consumed by hysteria, all-consuming laughter, and obsessions, especially with excrement.

His laughter was not frivolous; in his own words, it was catastrophic, an abyss, and terror.

I explained to him how his fascination with excrement marred his essential work. He claimed this was a deliberate terror device designed to shock.

But I said: 'It's loathsome to me and risks weakening your work. Instead of being admired for its deeper meaning or artistic value, your art may be dismissed as the product of a disturbed mind."

After a pause, her voice softens, and she murmurs, "Salvador is unlike anyone I've ever met. When I saw his work, I knew he was destined for greatness, but I realised he needed me to help him reach it.

He was terrified of his own genius, paralysed by doubt and insecurity.

I became his anchor, his shield. I took him by the hand and soothed him. I told him:

Let the world call you mad. Let them call you a fool. I will make sure they also call you a genius."

Do you ever feel burdened by the weight of that responsibility?

"Never. It is not a burden; it is a privilege. Salvador trusts me completely in a way that no one else ever has. He has let me take control, not just of his career but of our lives.

I negotiate with galleries, arrange exhibitions, and handle finances.

I ensure that his work is seen, celebrated, and sold. Without me, Salvador would be a forgotten eccentric. With me, he has become a legend."

Let's explore the world of the Surrealists, including André Breton, Max Ernst, and other key figures who formed the movement's core. Looking back, what do you think of them now?

"They were boys," she says dismissively, waving a hand as if brushing away a fly.

"Talented, yes, but still boys. Paul Éluard was my first poet, my first student of desire. He wrote me into his words, but I needed more than words.

Max Ernst painted me as his goddess, but he was too wild and free. I couldn't tame him like I tamed Dalí.

All of them played at being revolutionaries, but they couldn't handle a true revolutionary when they encountered one.

Breton especially hated me because I refused to play by his rules. He thought I was destroying Dalí by taking him away from the surrealist movement.

The truth is, Salvador and I had outgrown them. Surrealism never consisted of Breton and his petty little rules. It was about breaking boundaries and defying conventions.

Salvador is my destiny. His visions would be chaos without me, and his genius? It is mine to guide."

She leans forward, offering something between pride and defiance: "They hated me because I was a woman who refused to be silent or remain anonymous in the background, but they also envied me.

They coveted the power I had and the influence I wielded. Most of all, they resented that I did not need them.

You're interested in Muses. Let me tell you that being one is not about being passive. It is to challenge, provoke and inspire.

It is to see in someone else what they cannot see in themselves and to draw it out of them, no matter the cost.

That is what I do for Salvador. That is what I did for Paul and his poetry. And in doing so, I ensured my immortality. As long as their work is remembered, so will I be.

Do you know what the greatest tragedy of being a muse is? she asks, her voice barely above a whisper.

It is that you are always seen through someone else's eyes. People think they know me because they know Dalí or Éluard. But they don't know Gala. Not really. But that is as it should be.

Mystery is a powerful thing, no? Let them wonder. Let them speculate. Ultimately, the only person who truly knows Gala...is Gala.

I have become the living embodiment of surrealist ideals, the muse who defies convention, representing their dream world. No matter what they called me, I was intellectually and artistically free."

Gala, you are more than a Muse to Salvador. You are a manager, agent, and protector, and you regularly encourage him to return to painting. Is that not correct?

Another sharp intake of breath, and I know I'm pushing the limits of her patience. After a long pause, she answers her own question, almost as if whispering:

"What was I meant to do? We need the money. Dalí is just hanging out playing with willing young models, getting them to do orgasmic poses - and he gets a kick out of looking at them."

Well, Gala, aren't you a rich enough woman already? He's a famous worldwide artist, and his paintings command tremendous prices.

After another agonising pause, Gala frowns and finally replies, nearly in a whisper: "Enough money? Enough? What is enough? Salvador creates because he needs to.

Limits do not bind his genius, nor should it be stifled by the comfort of wealth. Each new painting, each brush stroke, is a triumph over mediocrity.

I challenge him because the world needs more of him. And perhaps, so do I."

Rising gracefully, Gala wraps her shawl around her shoulders and signals our conversation is ending.

Turning to me one last time with that unmistakable mix of confidence and enigma, she says in something close to a growl:

"Remember this about being a muse: you must be more than a reflection; you must be the light itself."

THE MUSE PERSPECTIVE

Gala Dalí played a revolutionary role. She evaded what history declared a muse meant.

She would not be reduced to a trivial footnote in the artist's creativity. Instead, she became a force of dynamism and action.

Her impact was wide-ranging. It influenced the art of her era and the idea of a muse.

In her interpretation of a muse, Gala was both partner and collaborator with one of the most mysterious creatives of the 20th century. She harnessed his eccentricity into a unified artistic identity.

Aware of his potential from an early age, she became his emotional anchor and the architect of his public image. As Dalí pointed out, "It is *mainly with your blood, Gala, that I paint my pictures.”*

She proved that a muse could be as much a creator as an artist.

While some critics have labelled her as domineering or opportunistic, Gala challenged the male-dominated artistic circles of the time.

Many contemporaries recognised her as a trailblazer. She broke down barriers for women in art, not just as artists but as equal and essential partners in the creative process.

Behind every masterpiece is a story. In Dalí's case, that story is Gala's - a story of vision, collaboration, and influence.

In her twilight years, Gala was addicted to sex and gambling. She was also permanently angry and fearful of losing her hold over Dalí.

As his muse, Gala could rightly claim:

“Without me, it would never have happened.”

NOTE: Gala died in 1982 and was buried in her castle, now open to the public as the Gala-Dalí Castle House Museum in Púbol, Spain. Salvador could not live without her and faded away in a few short years.

For an enjoyable, revelatory biography, find a copy of Wicked Lady: Salvador Dalí's Muse by Tim McGirk, Hutchinson, 1989.

More recently, Surreal by Michele Klein is an entertaining and readable work, published by Virago in 2025.

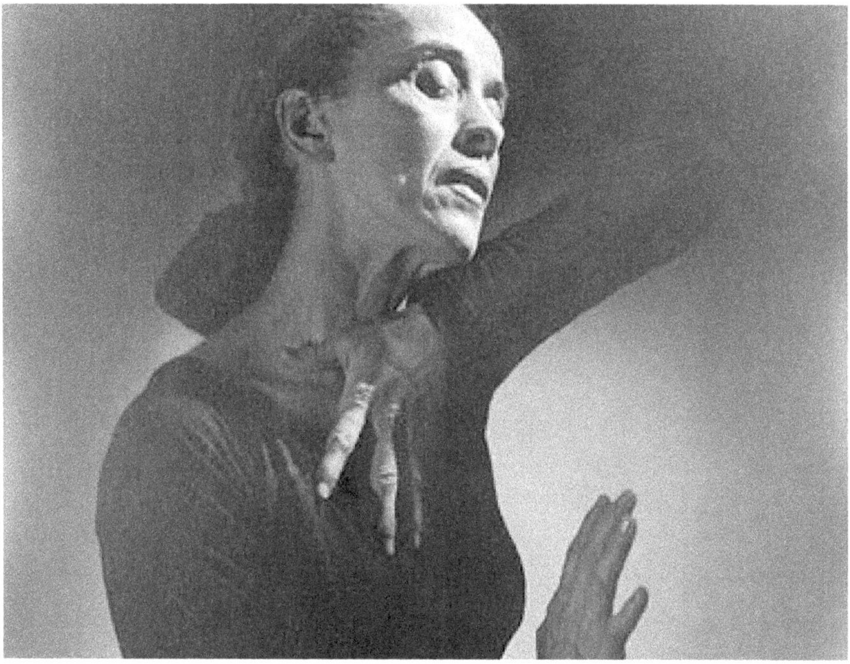

MARTHA GRAHAM

1894–1991

Martha Graham's dances revolutionised the art form. With her carefully selected, highly flexible dancers, she expanded the boundaries of classical ballet, making it more expressive and emotionally driven.

Graham was renowned for her innovative contraction and release method. In 1931, she founded the Martha Graham Dance Company and helped shape generations of dancers.

As a Muse, Graham inspired artists across various disciplines, including composers like Aaron Copland and sculptor Isamu Noguchi.

MARTHA GRAHAM

"If you want to be a mediocre dancer, that's your business. But you'll do it somewhere else, not in my studio."

These words of wisdom and confrontation from Graham during rehearsals underline her reputation for sometimes brutal honesty.

This is the woman I am about to meet. It's the start of the 1960s, and New York is now one of the most iconic cultural hubs of the decade.

The Martha Graham Dance Company's studio nestles deep in Manhattan, walled in by the sharp lines of brownstones and besieged by towering buildings.

As I step into the studio, it's an oasis in the frenetic city. This space enjoys ample sunlight, has high ceilings, and expansive windows.

Walls of mirrors help reflect light onto the polished wood floors, creating a soft glow and an open, warm ambience.

A framed statement by the studio management reads, "This is a place celebrating the art of movement."

It is not silent. There's the faint cadence of dancers moving, light footfalls, and the murmur of instructors leading them.

I'm guided to a corner and wait, soaking up the invisible creative energy surrounding me. With an understated yet undeniable presence, Martha Graham enters.

She's medium height, with her hair neatly pulled back yet retaining a natural wildness.

I watch as she moves towards me with the effortless grace of someone whose body has learned the language of poise from years of discipline. Her loose tunic and slacks are practical and straightforward.

Martha Graham, it's an honour to speak with you today. I'm pursuing my goal of exploring the role of Muse.

"Welcome, I am sure we have much to discuss. The role of Muse has many meanings for me."

I'd like to hear about your background. How did you come to dance? What initially drew you to it, Martha Graham?

"Just Martha will do. I'll try to explain how dance took over my life.

My family valued education, though not necessarily the arts. But just one moment changed everything. As a shy child full of curiosity, I was unsure of myself.

It wasn't until I was 14 that I saw Ruth St. Denis perform. It was as if a light had been switched on inside me. I didn't realise it then, but this was my first encounter with what would become my life's work.

It wasn't only the movement. It was also a way for the body to express emotion and tell a story without words.

I was fortunate to train at the Denishawn School under Ruth and Ted Shawn. Deep down, though, I knew I needed to break free from those traditions and move away from the constraints of older techniques.

I set out to find a language that speaks directly to the soul."

You were determined to create something new, to push the boundaries of dance. But how did your journey as a choreographer and teacher evolve?

"You know. Until I left Denishawn, I had never heard "choreographer" used to describe a maker of dances. There, you just made up dances.

Frankly, I never cared much for choreographing. It is a wonderfully big word that can cover many things.

Today, I seldom say, I am choreographing; I say, I am working.

The drive to innovate became my compass when contemporary dance began taking shape. Much of my focus was on breaking away from the rigid structures of ballet, and that was part of that rebellion.

I wanted to give voice to the elemental and primal emotions through the body. To me, dance is the soul's hidden language.

So, I adopted and cherished a rawness that contrasted sharply with the elegance of traditional ballet. That's when I developed two essential techniques.

The first was the 'contraction and release' technique, which links the body to its emotional and psychological core. The second technique was the concept of the Fall."

Yes, I've heard of this and even seen it being used. How does it work exactly?

 "The Fall manipulates the body's centre of gravity, allowing the dancers to explore the themes of weight and gravity in new ways."

Can any well-trained dancer execute your two fundamental techniques? Can you enlighten me on this?

"Ah, that's indeed the right question to ask! You must be exceptionally flexible, as exaggerated movements can be challenging and painful.

These techniques were initially developed in an all-female company, although they have since been expanded to include men.

It's also partly the basis for what is now called the Martha Graham

Dance Company.

That's when my work as a dance designer and a teacher truly began to take flight with a group of highly flexible dancers who shared my passion for the craft.

When dancers ask about my method, I usually say: 'You don't *think* about art. You *feel* it, you *live* it.'

When I trained, I ensured that I was always focused on the internal. I didn't care how I looked doing the movements. What mattered was why I was doing them.

Contractions and releases are not just physical actions. When dancers connect those inner feelings with the movement, they're no longer just performing; they live the dance. That's when the magic happens."

You've inspired many artists across various disciplines, and many consider you a Muse. Are you?

"Ah, now we come to your interesting question. Yes, being called a Muse is both a gift and a challenge. When I inspire others, the role is fluid, like a wind that stirs leaves, unseen but felt.

Once I established my company, the dynamic shifted, though. Now, my role as a Muse has become intentional. I am no longer merely an inspiration - I am a guide, a catalyst, a vessel through which others channel their creativity.

This responsibility deepened my connection to the creative force.

I could no longer dwell in the abstract. I had to embody the Muse fully, to live and breathe the art daily, so that others could draw from it.

Such a commitment has made me relentless and demanding, not for myself but for the art we created together.

Yet, the essence of the Muse remained unchanged. The Muse's role is to ignite an official or unofficial spark.

My company allowed me to fan that spark into a flame that burned brighter and reached farther than I ever could have foreseen."

Can you talk about a practical example of you deliberately acting as a Muse?

"One of the most profound experiences I've had as a Muse, or perhaps 'catalyst' is a better description, was with the composer Aaron Copland. He wrote the music for Appalachian Spring, one of my most cherished works.

I had a vision for what I wanted to convey, but Aaron brought his musical language to it, and we inspired each other. He showed me a new way to hear the music, just as I showed him a new way to see movement.

And there was Isamu Noguchi, a sculptor whose set designs for my works, like Cave of the Heart and Night Journey, added a new visual dimension.

His understanding of space and form was unlike any other. Together, we created works that transcended the limits of dance and sculpture."

Am I right that this was not just a professional, dance-based relationship?

"You're being too polite. It's hardly a secret that I had a blazing, exhausting and incredible romance with Isamu. Our relationship was highly creative and deeply conflicted.

He was attracted to my personality, but that had its downside, and with hindsight, my uncompromising nature often drove us apart."

You've also influenced so many dancers. Who are some of the performers you feel most connected to as a mentor or Muse?

"There are many, and each one has been such a gift. Merce Cunningham, for example. Though we took different paths, Merce moved toward abstraction in dance, and his work was profoundly shaped by the foundation I laid. There was always a deep respect between us, despite our differences.

José Limón was another, a torchbearer for modern dance who took what I started and made it his own. He had an unmatched artistry, and his understanding of my work helped bring it to life in ways I never could have imagined.

Then, of course, there's my Dance company. I've seen many young dancers grow, bringing fresh interpretations to my work. That's the beauty of reciprocity.

Teaching is not just about giving. It's about learning from each new generation.

It's humbling to see how my designs live on in the bodies of others, evolving in ways I never anticipated."

Your Dance company demonstrates the lasting power of your work. What is the most powerful aspect of being part of the dance community?

"It is ever-evolving, not static. It's a space where we challenge, push, and open up new possibilities. Unlike many art forms, dance has a vulnerability to it.

When a dancer steps on stage, they expose their body and soul. A kind of transformation happens, not just of the work, but of the dancers themselves.

I don't just want to teach them to perform my dances; I want to teach them to appreciate the artistry behind them. I want them to connect deeply with its essence and make it their own.

That's the beauty of the dance community. It's a living, breathing thing that grows far beyond the sum of its parts. To dance is sometimes to confront discomfort or ugliness."

You're known for doing just that: being direct and honest and living with an intensity that has proved magnetic but intimidating.

"That's a fair description. I am fully immersed in my world; art is my life, not just a career. It's a spiritual mission. I suppose you could say that my devotion to raw emotional energy helps define me.

I suffer from the divine dissatisfaction that drives artists never to settle. No artist is ever pleased. There's a blessed unrest that keeps us marching and makes us more alive than others."

You encouraged Copland to abandon his intellectualism and write from the heart. The result was a masterpiece.

"When I started, dance was still seen as a lesser art form beneath theatre or music.

I wanted to elevate it and show that it could speak to the soul in ways words and music couldn't. Dance is a complete language that expresses the most profound truths of the human condition.

If my work has done anything, it's helped shift how people view dance

Not as a mere aesthetic but as a powerful means of revealing something essential about ourselves and our place in the world. I'm proud to have contributed to that shift."

Yes, that is a very real achievement. Martha, could I now ask how

you see the future and what you will leave behind?

"I deeply respect the human spirit and its infinite capacity for invention. The body never lies. And if that is what I leave behind, I am more than content."

"Now, if you'll excuse me, I have a class due. It's been a pleasure speaking with you, and I wish you well with your Muse project. I'm glad to be part of it."

THE MUSE PERSPECTIVE

Martha Graham was a pioneering figure in modern dance and a Muse to countless artists across various disciplines.

Her radical approach to movement revolutionised dance and inspired generations through its focus on emotional expression and the power of the human form.

As a Muse, Graham inspired those who had nothing to do with dancing.

Louise Brooks, a film star famed for her "Bob" or "Flapper Bob" chin-length haircut, which became iconic during the Jazz Age, claimed: *'I learned to act by studying Martha Graham's dancing'.*

Bette Davis, one of the greatest silver screen icons, said Graham taught her how to use her body expressively. This skill significantly influenced her acting career: *'Every time I climbed a flight of stairs in films… it was Graham step by step'.*

Graham's illustrious students included Gregory Peck, Woody Allen, and Madonna. Others included Rudolf Nureyev, ballet star Margot Fonteyn, actress, singer, and dancer Liza Minnelli, and many more.

Graham's impact on fellow dancers was profound within and outside her company. Many choreographers and performers adapted her "contract and release" principles.

She also sparked filmmakers' imaginations. She produced cinematic body language that echoed her groundbreaking use of physicality to convey meaning.

Painters and sculptors found a new language for her work, which captured the human form in motion.

Her legacy further reverberated in literature. Writers saw in her dances ways to express the human form in motion, prompting them to think about new ways to tell stories.

Her technique is widely regarded as the "cornerstone" of contemporary American dance and is taught worldwide.

It remains the "hallmark" style of modern concert dance; its movement vocabulary is familiar to almost all professional contemporary dancers.

As a Muse, she made people feel valued and was intolerant of self-absorbed or self-destructive attitudes.

A young dancer kept apologising for her mistakes. Graham called a halt to the class and said: "Stop apologising for being alive! You have the right to take up space. Use it"

This wasn't just the dancer in Graham speaking; it was a philosophy by which this marvellous Muse lived.

NOTE: Martha Graham shares her approach: https://tinyurl.com/338nsjmx

Blood Memory: An Autobiography by Martha Graham, published by Sceptre in 1999, is an excellent read. The opening alone grabs your attention with the stark assertion:

"I am a dancer."

LOUIS ARMSTRONG

1901-1971

Louis Armstrong blossomed from a wayward youth into a giant whose image towered over a vast slice of American music history.

Armstrong recast jazz not as a primarily team or band activity. Instead, the solo jazz artist became a gravel-voiced singer, virtuoso trumpet player, and dynamic performer.

Armstrong inspired musicians and audiences worldwide, and his influence extended beyond racial and cultural boundaries.

Louis Armstrong, known as "Satchmo" or "Pops," had a five-decade career that makes it nearly impossible to sum up or fully encapsulate the artist.

His monumental contribution to jazz and influence extended far beyond playing the cornet.

LOUIS ARMSTRONG

This place we're meeting couldn't be better, and it's Armstrong's personal choice. It's 1955, and this Jazz genius is in his early 50s.

He's agreed to talk about his role as a muse. He remains healthy, vibrant, and active.

For our conversation, he's proposed a rendezvous at this cosy jazz club in New Orleans.

I've found a discreet table at the back with just two chairs and anticipate the arrival of a musical legend at any minute.

I wonder what Satchmo might like to drink. Maybe a Sazerac, the quintessential New Orleans cocktail made with rye whiskey or cognac.

Or perhaps he'd prefer a mint julep, a mix of bourbon, sugar, mint, and crushed ice; it's smooth, stylish, and a great nod to Southern charm.

A four-piece band starts tuning up to play traditional New Orleans jazz, which should make Armstrong feel at home. Hopefully, it won't drown out our conversation.

And here he is! He offers his signature warm smile and is dressed sharply but comfortably in a three-piece suit with a subtly patterned tie.

His iconic white handkerchief peeks from his top pocket, and he carries his well-travelled trumpet case, which he carefully places beside him.

Welcome, Satchmo. Thank you for taking the time to discuss being a muse. Can I get you a drink or a mint julep?

"It's good to meet you. I'm sure lookin' forward to our talk about being a muse, though I don't think about it often. Just a coffee for me, thanks, black."

Thankfully, the band has now gone for a drink, so with luck, it should stay quiet for a while. With the coffee in place and the basics out of the way, I ask:

Can you tell me about your childhood here in New Orleans and how it shaped your love for music?

"Sure thing. Yes, New Orleans is where it all began, baby! It was like the music was in the air, in the water, in your bones. Comin' up wasn't easy, not by a long shot.

I was born near the Back O'Town section of New Orleans. I didn't have much, just my mama, sister, and the streets. My daddy left early on, and we had to make do.

I sold newspapers, delivered coal, and even scavenged food sometimes. But through it all, there was music.

Then I got into trouble and landed in the Waif's Home. That's when I connected with my first real horn."

Could you tell me about this trouble and why you were sent to that home for children?

"Gee, I hardly ever talk about that stuff! Still, I'll tell you like it was. It was New Year's 1912, and I was eleven years old, celebrating in the streets of New Orleans.

In the thrill of the evening, I got hold of my stepfather's .38 revolver. I just wanted to join in, so I fired it up like the others were doin'.

Unfortunately, the police didn't think much of what I had done, and I was sent to the Coloured Waifs' Home for Boys, a reform school for troubled youth. At the time, it seemed like punishment. Then, there was this miracle in disguise.

In the school band, I got a music education and man, it was a blast. I'd once had a crappy tin horn and used to wonder how I would do blowing a real horn.

I saw this little cornet in a pawn shop window for five dollars and managed to buy it after several weeks of saving. It was all dirty, but with help, I got it cleaned up and shiny.

But man, when I got my hands on that real cornet in the Home, it was like findin' my voice.

Being a musician taught me discipline and gave me a goal. The school band leader discovered something in me and encouraged me to practice. I owe him a lot."

One rash move on New Year's Eve turned into the start of everything."

"Yeah, where I lived was a bad neighbourhood. The parades, the brass bands, those lines of people, they called out to me.

Even in lean times, that music made you feel alive. And let me tell ya, when I heard King Oliver play the first time? Man. That was it. I knew what I wanted to do."

Before we discuss that, may I ask about something that puzzles people? How did you come to be called Satchmo?

"It was like this. New Orleans was where nicknames were the thing to have and give. I accumulated several. I doubt you've heard of them, but one was Sachelmouth, which I suppose was about me talking a lot.

When I first went to England in 1932, an Englishman who met me at the boat shook my hand, saying: "Hello, Satchmo." Man, I flipped. That was the first time hearing this name, and I've been Satchmo ever since."

That's a great story. Could you please tell me about King Oliver, one of your earliest musical influences, and how he inspired you?

"Man, that was somethin' else. Chicago was hoppin'. In 1922, King Oliver, my idol, mentor and father figure who liked my playin', wired me to come to Chicago.

Four days after my twenty-fifth birthday, I packed a small bag containing a trout sandwich my mother had fixed and caught the evening train. King Oliver and his wife found me a place to stay at a boarding house run by a friend of Oliver's called Filo.

The Olivers taught me the ways of Chicago. Playing with Oliver felt like stepping into the big leagues.

From that cat, I learned how to lead a band, play with others, and shine when it was my time.

And those crowds! They were wild for the music. It made me realise just how powerful jazz could be."

So, how did growing up in New Orleans affect your approach to music and life?

"Growin' up in a place like that, you know, you see life in all the colour, the good, the bad, the beautiful. It toughened me up, but it also gave me heart.

The people there had so much spirit in their lives, which I think I tried to capture in my music.

I wanted every note to tell a story, making you feel something, just as the streets of New Orleans made me feel.

Yes, you certainly did that! And how did your experiences recording the Hot Five and Hot Seven sessions change your perspective on jazz?

"Man, those sessions were magic. That's where I really showed what jazz could be. We weren't just playin' tunes; we were creatin' somethin' new, finding our way and experimenting.

It taught me that jazz was not only about the notes, but also about the feeling and the story that went with it. That took the soloist and put him under a spotlight, changing everything for jazz."

Relationships usually make a big difference to artists, Satchmo. What about yours?

"How d'yer mean?"

I understand you're with your fourth wife! How have these wives affected your development as an artist?

"Oh, man! That's not something I expected to talk about! You see, all my wives knew that the trumpet came first. They each influenced my performance and how I supported others.

Daisy Parker was with me in my early life and helped me focus on my need for independence. Lil Hardin played a significant role in my growing success and took a keen interest in my performance.

She didn't think much of my playing second fiddle to King Oliver. Alpha Smith, my third wife, offered stability but was mainly interested in furs and diamonds, so naturally, we had problems balancing my personal and professional life.

Lucille, my wife since 1942, is so supportive and allows me to make sense of and pursue my roles as mentor, muse, or whatever you call them.

I guess all those experiences helped me pour more truth into the music."

You've been most generous with your time, Satchmo. Can I take up a bit more and focus on being a muse? What does being a muse mean to you as an artist?

"That's sure somethin', huh? To me, it's like being a light. You light somethin' in somebody else, give 'em a little piece of yourself, your heart, soul, ideas and watch 'em grow into somethin' beautiful.

It ain't about tellin' folks what to do, no, sir. It's about lettin' 'em feel somethin' true and makin' 'em believe they can turn it into somethin' all their own. That's what keeps the music swingin', baby!"

Of the many musicians you've worked with, is there a special one you've been a muse to, inspiring and steering them in new directions?

"Aw, man, I've been lucky to work with many cats.

Take my boy Dizzy Gillespie - trumpeter, bandleader, composer, teacher, and singer. Diz once said he wouldn't have been the musician he is if he hadn't heard me blowin' that horn.

And then there's Miles Davis, the jazz trumpeter, bandleader, and composer. He says, "I made him want to play, plain and simple."

I set out to steer nobody, you dig? But doin' my thing, playin' from the heart, seemed to stir somethin' in folks. That's a blessing."

What sort of things do you tell them leading to their development?

"I don't hold back, man. I tell 'em the truth, baby. Don't just play the notes - live inside 'em. Feel every single one, even if it's just a low-down blues or a little ol' love song.

I say, *'Play it like you mean it, or don't play it at all.'* And sometimes I'd show 'em, not just tell 'em, like with my phrasing. Folks like Bing

Crosby picked up on how I'd stretch a note or play around the beat. They took that and ran with it, man.

Oh, they've said some sweet things, that's for sure.

Take Dizzy Gillespie. Dizzy is the real deal and practically invented bebop. He said I was the king who opened the door for everybody else.

Miles Davis, the band leader, trumpeter and composer, called me his idol. And Ella Fitzgerald, that angel, said she'd listen to my records to learn. Hearin' that, whew, it's humblin'.

I just played what I loved, you know? I didn't think it would mean so much to so many."

Let's try to tie this muse thing down even further, please. What do you think makes an influential muse?

"Well, now, they gotta have somethin' that grabs folks that makes them feel. You gotta give folks the truth, even if it's messy or even hurts.

And you gotta be generous with it, too. You can't be holdin' back your light if it can help somebody else shine. Most of all, you gotta love what you do and love it so much that it spills over and gets into the people around you."

How have your muses helped you to do the same for others?

"Aw, I had my muses, all right. King Oliver, like I said. That man taught me how to blow, lead, and carry myself.

And folks like Bessie Smith and Ma Rainey, the blues singer. We called her 'Mother of the Blues'. She showed what it means to put your whole heart into a song. They gave me so much, and I guess I just wanted to pass it on, you know? Keep the chain goin'."

You sure do that! How does it feel to know your work has inspired generations of musicians?

"Oh, man, it feels like the greatest thing in the world. To think somethin' I played, somethin' I sang, could reach people I've never met long after I'm gone? That's somethin' else.

It's like leavin' a little piece of yourself behind, somethin' that keeps on talkin' to folks keeps on makin' 'em feel. And that's all I ever wanted, to move people."

There are hardly any major venues left where you haven't played. Is there a particular audience or city that gets your juices flowing more than others?

"People love the music everywhere, and that inspires. But Paris, oh man, Paris is something special.

They serve jazz as if it were high art. Going back there and playing that was deep. It felt like coming home."

I know that staying grounded has also been important to you. How do you remain true to yourself as a musician while constantly innovating?

"It's about respect, baby. Respect for where you come from, who came before you, and the music that made you. You gotta honour the tradition, but you also gotta find your voice.

That's what jazz is about, takin' something old and making it new."

Nearly a decade ago, you formed the Louis Armstrong All-Stars. What does this group mean to you?

"The All-Stars is my way of gettin' back to basics. Small groups, tight arrangements, real personal music. We have some of the best players around, like Jack Teagarden and Barney Bigard. Playing with them is pure joy.

It reminds me of why I fell in love with jazz in the first place. Oh, man, we're playin' all over the world, bringin' that swing to folks everywhere.

We just finished a killer show in Europe, and let me tell you, they love the music over there just as much as they do back home.

Every night's a new adventure with this band, Trummy on trombone, Edmond Hall blowin' that clarinet and Velma singin' her heart out.

Did ya know she started as a chorus girl and dancer - doin' acrobatic splits right on stage? I loved having her around. It's like a family, you dig? We keep each other swingin'."

Trummy Young is a fantastic jazz trombonist, but he's far more than that, isn't he?

"Sure thing. He's a strong singer and composer. Do yer' know Trummy co-wrote and sang the hit song T'ain't What You Do (It's the Way That You Do It), which is now a swing classic."

Can you describe the moment when you realised you'd achieved worldwide fame?

"I'll tell ya, the first time I played in Europe and saw those crowds going crazy for the music is when it hit me. But fame, man, it's just a word.

What mattered was seeing people's faces light up when I played. That's the real prize."

Was there ever a time when you doubted your path in music? If so,

what kept you going?

"There were tough times, sure, but the music always pulled me through. When things got hard, I'd think about the people who believed in me – King Oliver, Mr. Davis, my mama. And then I pick up my horn and play my way through it."

Finally, Satchmo, what advice would you give young musicians trying to find their voice?

"Be yourself, baby. Don't try to copy anyone else, but learn from the greats. Discover your sound and way of tellin' your story. And always play from the heart.

Oh, and one more thing! If you're going on the road, as one of my jazz buddies once said, you only need to take one thing: a toothbrush and a picture of Louis Armstrong!"

Our time is up, and this masterful entertainer retrieves his instrument case, grins at me once more and exits stage left.

THE MUSE PERSPECTIVE

The journey of Louis Armstrong is pure alchemy - from the streets of New Orleans to the heights of global music."

He had a significant impact on individuals and served as a muse.

His defection from New Orleans to Chicago was an epochal jailbreak. He had left behind the collective style of New Orleans for the swift, virtuoso style that contributed to the jazz scene of the 1920s.

As a muse, his approach to advancing the soloist role in jazz has influenced generations of improvisers to discover their own voices.

Armstrong rewrote the meaning of performance - his blend of technical mastery and an infectious personality connected with audiences everywhere.

His trumpet solos and scat singing became master classes in improvisation and expression, influencing artists in other genres.

Over the years of practising his writing hobby, Armstrong also developed a prose voice as distinctive as his musical voice.

His literary efforts are not mere meanderings of a busy performer or rock star. They shed fresh light on the evolution of jazz.

As a cultural ambassador, Armstrong also broke barriers, bringing jazz to audiences on tours across Europe, Africa, and Asia.

His music spoke a universal language that transcended racial and cultural boundaries.

Despite facing discrimination, he kept his spirit alive, becoming both an inspiration and a bright ray of hope for those he interacted with.

NOTE: Louis Armstrong has been the subject of countless biographies and music histories. You may be interested in:

Louis Armstrong, in His Own Words: Selected Writings, Oxford University Press, 1999.

Also, take a look at this vivid and fascinating portrait, Satchmo: The Genius of Louis Armstrong, by Gary Giddins, Da Capo Press; Reprint edition 2001

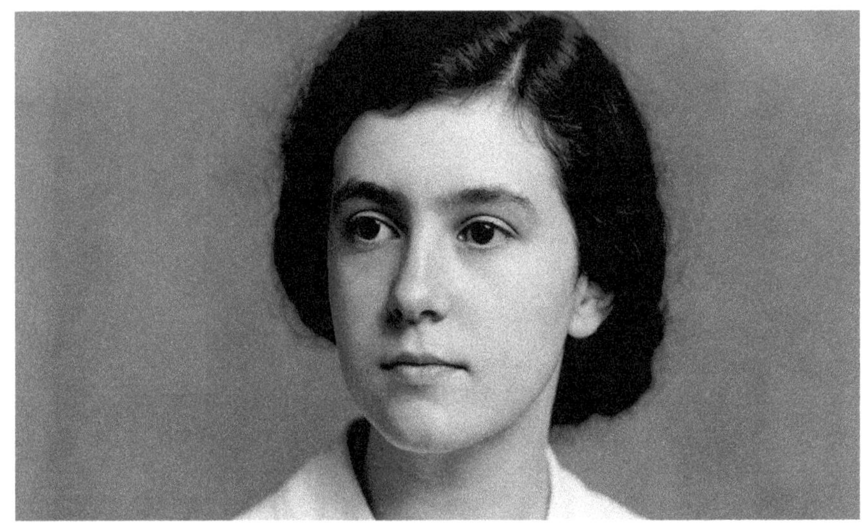

EILEEN O'SHAUGHNESSY

1905-1945

Eileen O'Shaughnessy was a thoughtful, sharp, and compassionate person, and a key figure in George Orwell's life and work.

A poet and intellectual, she balanced her passions against her role as Orwell's confidante, editor, and partner.

Her impact resonates through Orwell's best books, despite her usual lack of credit.

Whatever the truth, history is now viewing Eileen O'Shaughnessy with more respect, recognising her as a classic, self-effacing and influential Muse.

Without her interventions, support, and subtle insights, Orwell would never have achieved the fame he eventually achieved.

EILEEN O'SHAUGHNESSY

The lane to The Stores Cottage in Wallington is quiet, save for the occasional rustle of hens pecking near the low stone wall. The cottage is modest, red-bricked, with a tiled roof.

Its small front garden is bordered by a tangle of hedgerows and a worn footpath leading to the door. Smoke curls from the chimney, carrying the faint scent of burning wood and something else - perhaps stew or George Orwell's pipe tobacco.

It is 1938, and I'm about to meet Eric Blair's partner. Blair's publishing name was George Orwell, the third pseudonym he considered using.

He is known as Orwell in literary and political circles, although not widely recognised.

But I am not here for Orwell; I am here for Eileen O'Shaughnessy, his wife and Muse. I knock one time, then pause and knock again.

There's a momentary struggle from inside, and the door bursts open. Eileen is small and extremely thin, with sharp eyes and an ink smudge on her fingers.

She sizes me up with an inscrutable look before cracking a wry smile.

Even though I have arranged to meet her rather than her husband, she still says:

"You must be here to see Eric, but I'm afraid you're out of luck. He's off playing at being a farmer. That or he's terrorising the chickens again, whichever comes first."

I explain again why I am here. She moves aside and gestures for me to come in. The room is orderly in a disordered way.

Books teeter on every surface. Sheets of paper marked by Orwell's soaring scrawl inhabit the space like literary landmines. A battered typewriter rests on a distressed wooden table.

The entire place smells of ink, tea and damp wool. The spare living space embodies the austerity of their lives but is also crammed with artefacts of intellectual endeavour.

Pushing a few papers aside, Eileen gestures for me to sit. She is genial and brisk. She serves me tea, pouring it into mismatched cups as I look around.

This isn't just a home - it's the crucible of Orwell's ideas. And Eileen - she's at the centre of this, whether she admits it or not.

With an amused look, she passes me a cup and sits in the chair across from me. "So, what exactly do you want to know? I had supposed you were here about Eric, but you might find I have a few things of my own to say!"

No, I'm not here mainly about him, Eileen; I'm here for you and your role as a Muse. Can you tell me about your childhood and how it influenced your perspective on the world?

"My childhood in South Shields was happy enough. Though it was unremarkable. Growing up, I had a grounding in practical matters.

My father was a doctor, and I saw how much his work required intellect and compassion. It taught me to value a sharp mind tempered by kindness."

You, too, must have a sharp mind. I know you won a scholarship to Oxford and studied English Literature. How did the Oxford experience influence you?

"I was drawn to the beauty of language and how literature captures the complexities of human emotion.

Oxford was exhilarating - a place where thought and debate were currency. It sharpened my intellect and gave me confidence.

In 1934, I published a dystopian poem titled "End of the Century 1984." Still, even then, I knew women were seen as second-class scholars."

The themes of your poem and Orwell's book are similar; did he borrow the title for his famous nineteen-eighty-four?

"Maybe, or perhaps my poem planted the seed. We'll probably never know, and I am more than happy with his choice.

You clearly got a great deal from Oxford and enjoyed your time there.

"I loved it and desperately wanted to stay and teach. I'd hoped to get a first. When I didn't, it seemed like the ground had been removed from beneath my feet.

I lost confidence and felt it wasn't worth putting writing at the centre of my life.

I did many things that had nothing to do with poetry or academic writing. So, I left university and spent a term at a girls' boarding school.

I read aloud to the elderly Dame Elizabeth Cadbury, of Quaker chocolate-making fame, and delivered lectures at the Workers' Educational Association. Later, I started a secretarial business, but it never made much money.

Then I met Eric and finally knew what I needed to do.

What Eric liked about me was my independent mind, my gift for storytelling, and my ability to prick the absurdities of those around us.

Most of all, Eric was drawn to what he saw as a decent human being. This is a quality he would most wish to have himself."

How would you describe your intellectual pursuits outside of helping with Orwell's work?

"I suppose I am less an originator and more an organiser of ideas.

I love poetry and psychology and find joy in making sense of things, whether by editing or simply offering a different perspective.

My creativity lies in seeing connections where others might not. I've always considered myself someone who fosters creativity in others. It's a form of artistry, though a quieter one."

Well, Eileen, it confirms your role as a Muse, which, as I've said, is why I'm here. What first attracted you to Eric, or rather George Orwell, as a person and writer?

"His honesty. There's something disarming about someone who speaks their mind so plainly. As a writer, he has a way of stripping away pretence to get to the truth. I admire that deeply."

You've doubtless read Orwell's early works, and I wonder what you see in his writing that others might miss?

"There's a tenderness beneath the sharpness of his critiques. People often see him as hard-edged, but he's full of compassion for the downtrodden. It's just that his compassion is expressed through anger at injustice."

What are some ways you two intellectually inspire and challenge each other?

"We have endless discussions about politics, philosophy, and literature.

I feel like we challenge each other's perspectives. He counterbalances my optimism, and I temper his pessimism. It's a good balance."

Let's talk about your contributions to Orwell's work. Do you feel what you offer him is often unrecognised?

"I don't mind being behind the scenes. It's not about recognition but about helping Eric create something meaningful.

But yes, I suppose it can feel lonely to give so much and see your name left out."

How do you go about critiquing or editing Orwell's writing?

"I read everything he writes. Sometimes, it's several drafts. My role is to point out where he is being too dense or where he needs to clarify his thoughts.

I also argue with him about his ideas, which he appreciates, even if he pretends not to.

Sometimes, I suggest that he simplify the language to make it more accessible. He grumbles about it, of course, but he makes the changes."

Do you ever feel that Orwell's writing is collaborative or that he works best alone?

"Eric prefers flying solo, but cannot resist reaching out. He complains about the interference, but can't help himself covertly. It is collaborative, but not the old school way."

So, is there something about Orwell personally that makes it difficult to cooperate creatively?

"Absolutely! He can be incredibly single-minded and stubborn. But I think that's what makes him a genius. He requires someone to bring him down to earth, which I attempt to do. It's a constant juggle. "

I do practical things so he can concentrate. However, I do my best to keep my passions alive through reading and friendships. Still, there are moments when his needs take precedence."

Can you give an example of that happening?

"Certainly. For example, when the outside lav flooded, muck poured over the seat and into the box. Eric had to write, and his sensitivity meant he couldn't bring himself to do anything about it.

There wasn't money for a plumber, so I donned his waders and cleared it with garden gloves and a bucket."

Apart from what you call 'sensitivities', are there other aspects of Orwell's personality that make it hard to work alongside him?

"With Eric, there is always the unexpected. For instance, one day in 1936, he entered the kitchen while I was washing up.

Then, as casually as if he was popping out for cigarettes, he said: *'I thought I'd go to Spain to fight for the POUM militia of the Spanish communist party.'*

At least I knew what he was talking about. He meant the revolutionary Marxist and anti-Stalinist communist party in Spain. The militia was active during the Civil War."

How did you react to this sudden decision?

"I said I thought it was a good idea and said I'm sure we could be helpful.

He said: *'We? But I'll be at the front; there'd be nothing for you to do.'*

I didn't believe him, and the next year, I followed him out to Barcelona. Within three months, Eric was shot in the throat and had to be treated in Barcelona.

He was lucky to be alive, although his voice was affected for quite some time.

After the Stalinist repression against the POUM began, we fled, narrowly escaping arrest. With the help of contacts, we crossed France and returned to England."

It must have been terrifying, and he was fortunate to have you by his side during such a critical time.

"I think he was glad to have me there, though he didn't approve of my coming to Spain."

Due to the current situation in Europe, you are facing political and social turmoil. How is the problem affecting your thinking and your relationship with Orwell?

"It's making everything feel urgent. We both recognise the need to fight against oppression, although we approach it in different ways.

I think the turmoil brings us closer in some ways and adds strain in others."

Do you consider yourself a Muse to Eric in the traditional sense, or do you see your role as more collaborative and mutual?

"Yes, I see it as collaborative, even if he doesn't always see it that way! A Muse inspires but also challenges. I think I do both for Eric. Just as he does for me."

How do you feel about Orwell's sometimes bleak view of the world? Does your perspective differ from his?

"That's a good question. I often feel Eric focuses too much on the darkness.

I try to remind him of the small joys and the goodness in people. He listens, but I'm unsure I have ever changed his mind."

Eric seems to be demanding a lot of your time and attention. Do you ever feel that Eric's political and literary ambitions overshadow your contribution to the partnership?

Eileen closes her eyes as though overcome by memories: "Yes, often. But I understand his drive.

It's not easy to forgive and forget such instances, but I always know that what matters is his work."

How would you want your own contributions to Orwell's legacy to be remembered?

"As someone who helped him see the world a bit more clearly. I want to think my influence lives in the pages of his work, even if my name doesn't."

Eileen, you continue to sacrifice for Eric's career, always putting his wishes and needs before your own.

Is it worth it?

A long pause follows as Eileen considers this challenging confrontation. Finally, she briefly nods: "Yes, it isn't easy. Helping him create something lasting gives my life a sense of purpose, a reason for being.

What advice would you give to anyone else who supports or inspires a creative partner today?

Isn't that what Muses are for? If you're going to support or inspire a creative partner, be patient, but don't lose yourself in their work as I have often done. A true partnership is about mutual support, not self-erasure."

THE MUSE PERSPECTIVE

Eileen O'Shaughnessy transcended the role of Muse. She was Orwell's intellectual collaborator, profoundly influencing his work.

Her incisive judgment and editing helped hone Orwell's thinking, especially in Animal Farm and other polemics.

Her background in psychology also deepened Orwell's insight into human behaviour and power dynamics.

Eileen has always been an unseen woman, eclipsed and relegated to the dusty, forgotten pages of history. She was a victim, a captive of Orwell's desperation for success as a writer.

He rarely mentioned Eileen by name or acknowledged the depth of her insight and quiet devotion throughout his literary endeavours.

The male gaze, reinforced by biographical bias, has left Eileen's trail faint and nearly erased from view.

However, her role as Muse reminds us that often, behind history's most celebrated figures are individuals whose influences help guide the trajectory of that person's creations.

NOTE: For an insightful and compelling account of Eileen's life and her influence on Orwell, try Wifedom: Mrs Orwell's Invisible Life by Anna Funder (Viking, 2023)

SIMONE DE BEAUVOIR

1908-1986

Simone de Beauvoir was not merely a philosopher and writer but a muse of ideas, rebellion, and transformation. A foundational figure in existentialist thought, her works, most notably The Second Sex, in which she asked, 'What is a woman?' challenged the foundations of gender, autonomy, and freedom.

As a muse, De Beauvoir was neither passive nor a mere companion to her fellow philosopher, Jean-Paul Sartre; she helped to shape the philosophical landscape of the 20th century, inspiring generations to rethink what it means to exist, love, and be free.

SIMONE DE BEAUVOIR

Paris in 1949 is still emerging from the shadow of war. The river Seine reflects the pale winter afternoon light, and the streets are, once more, full of people.

My meeting with Simone de Beauvoir will be in this small library tucked inside a Left Bank publishing house, where manuscripts, philosophy texts, and political pamphlets fill the shelves.

This intimate and intellectual space mirrors her life as a philosopher, novelist, feminist, and, crucially, a muse of ideas. Though she had already helped reshape contemporary thought, her journey as an intellectual force is still unfolding.

The library smells of ink and what seems like paper dust. The early evening pavements of Paris outside echo with the sounds of students, philosophers, and possibly revolutionaries. Inside these hushed walls, though, it feels like an intellectual oasis.

Seated beside an overflowing stack of newly printed copies of The Second Sex, she glances up, her cigarette idly smouldering in the ashtray beside her.

She is striking, though not conventionally beautiful. Her dark brown hair, drawn back into a simple, elegant chignon, reveals high cheekbones and a sharp, intelligent face.

She wears a navy-blue blouse, and hanging on the back of her chair is a brown tweed jacket, slightly worn at the elbows. She has no jewellery, only a simple leather-strapped watch peeking beneath her cuff.

Good afternoon, Mademoiselle de Beauvoir. Thank you for agreeing to ...

"If you don't mind, Mademoiselle is meaningless to me, just as Madame would be. I prefer my name, Simone. Titles belong to outdated conventions. Formalities are unnecessary between thinking minds."

Thank you, Simone. I have long admired your work and am here to discuss something about which you seem to have strong views.

Her head nods slightly, a flicker of amusement crossing her features: "Yes, let's continue to speak English; I am delighted as I rarely have the opportunity to speak it, except when I travel.

I love its rhythm, though I fear my French accent is rather strong."

She gestures toward the chair opposite her. "Sit, then. Let us talk. I much prefer a discussion to a monologue."

She exhales a final plume of smoke before stubbing out the cigarette and folding her hands neatly on the table. Her gaze sharpens, expectant. "Now - where shall we begin?"

My reason for being here, Simone, is my interest in the role of the muse. Would you ever have considered yourself a muse to anyone?

"No, women have had to destroy the role to free themselves. The traditional idea of a muse has often reduced women to mere inspiration for male genius.

If I have inspired others, it is not by sitting prettily and providing emotional fuel but by engaging intellectually, arguing, and disrupting. Such behaviour is not traditionally associated with being a muse."

You seem to suggest, Simone, that the concept of a muse has historically been limiting for women. Have I got that right?

"Absolutely. The moment she shapes ideas, she ceases to be a muse and becomes something else: a thinker, a writer, and a rebel.

Let me put it this way. A muse who creates is no longer a muse but a force of her own. There is a difference between being an influence and being a catalyst. I have been the latter.

A muse inspires; a catalyst provokes. I have always preferred to provoke."

Given your closeness to your long-term friend Jean-Paul Sartre, I wonder if you have ever felt like a muse to him. Or is your relationship always an equal exchange?

"Our relationship is built on intellectual reciprocity. I am not his muse but his thought partner. We debate, we argue, and we build ideas together.

If I am in any sense a muse, then he is mine as well. But I can tell you the word doesn't capture the ferocity of our exchanges."

What is your reaction to people who see you as Sartre's "companion" rather than a philosopher in your own right?

"It is contempt. I realise the world is more comfortable seeing me as an extension of Sartre than acknowledging that I stand beside him, not behind him.

But I never waste energy on such people. My work speaks louder than their assumptions."

Yes, I agree. So, would you say that philosophy and literature tend to be driven by the need for muses? Or is inspiration purely an internal process?

"It's a good point. Philosophy and literature need tension, not muses. They need unsettled questions and contradictions demanding resolution. A muse that merely sits silently is useless to either."

Do you think perhaps existentialism offers a way to redefine the role of a muse as something more autonomous?

"Absolutely. Existentialism rejects fixed roles. It insists that we define ourselves through action.

A muse who merely inspires is stagnant. An existentialist muse, if we can call such a person that, is in motion, evolving, and challenging.

In that sense, existentialism liberates the muse from silence and becomes a creator." She pauses for a moment and takes another cigarette. Looking thoughtful, she lights it and gazes at me, waiting for my next question.

Well, Simone, can I turn to some of your writing now? For example, how much of your first novel, She Came to Stay, was autobiographical?

"Much of it is autobiographical, but not all. The novel reflects my experiences, but it is not a diary.

I used my relationship with Sartre and Olga Kosakiewicz, the young student we took under our intellectual and emotional wing.

I transformed that framework into something more significant: exploring freedom, possession, and existential choice."

The emotional and psychological dynamics you describe in the novel seem to mirror real-life tensions from this complex triangular relationship.

"That is an astute observation. Through the novel, I questioned how freedom, possession, and relationships shape our existence.

It was not simply a story but an examination of how people construct their identities through choices and interactions with others"

Your philosophy suggests that emotions cannot be separated from our choices. Those who claim to live free of constraints must still confront the realities of human complexity. So, can a muse escape the societal constraints you describe in The Second Sex?

"Only if she ceases to be a muse in the traditional sense. The world does not easily allow women to be both admired and autonomous.

To escape constraint, she must redefine herself - not as an inspiration, but as an agent of her own making."

Do you ever struggle with being seen as a woman rather than simply a writer?

"I get frustrated when men dismiss my ideas by saying, 'You think this because you're a woman.' As if my reasoning is dictated by my sex rather than by logic and truth. But my answer is simple: 'I think this because it is true.

Yet, I cannot turn the argument back on them. I cannot say, 'And you think the contrary because you are a man.' Why? Because being a man is considered the universal norm.

A man is not required to justify his position as a 'male thinker'. He is simply a thinker. A man represents humanity, while a woman is always seen as particular, subjective, and separate.

Yes, women's work is always categorised differently, as if a separate standard must weigh it.

I do not want to be read as a 'woman philosopher' - I want to be read as a philosopher. But the world is not ready for that. It still isn't."

You have always been so incredibly productive. Do you ever feel pulled in too many directions between writing novels, philosophy, and memoirs?

"Constantly. But that is my nature. My work is not separate from my life; it's an extension. When I write philosophy, I must ground it in lived experience.

When I write fiction, I cannot help but engage with ideas. These forms are not competing forces. There are different ways of exploring the same questions.

I do not seek balance. I seek truth, and truth is never confined to a single genre. Passion, not discipline, is the driving force."

Your writing has always covered a large territory. What is the most complex philosophical idea you ever wrestled with?

"The question of whether absolute freedom is possible. Sartre argues that we are condemned to be free. That we always have a choice.

But I see that freedom is not so simple. We are shaped by our histories, our societies, and the invisible structures that limit our choices before we even make them.

Women, for instance, are told we are free. Yet, our lives are still constrained by expectations that we do not create. Even I, who preach freedom, have to admit its limits.

The challenge is not simply to claim freedom but to dismantle the conditions that restrict it."

If you could rewrite The Second Sex today, would you change anything?

"Perhaps particular historical examples, as the world keeps changing. But my central argument remains unchanged.

Women are still caught in structures that shape them before they even get to understand the word 'freedom.'

From birth, they are conditioned to play a role, conform, and believe their destiny lies in serving others. They are still judged by how they fit into ideals imposed by men, whether as wives, mothers, objects of desire, or symbols of morality.

They are still expected to sacrifice their ambitions, bodies, and voices for love, children, and society.

The structures of oppression adapt to each generation, disguising themselves as choice and progress. But a choice made under pressure is not genuinely free.

My words remain relevant until these fundamental structures are dismantled, not merely reformed. In many ways, the world has confirmed my arguments rather than disproven them."

In your opinion, what will be the most enduring impact of The Second Sex?

"I like to think it has made the oppression of women impossible to ignore. Before, it was an unspoken truth, something accepted as 'natural.'

The book exposes it as a deliberate construction that keeps women secondary.

More than that, it has given language to a struggle that had existed in silence. Women who felt uneasy, constrained, and stifled but could not say why now have the words to define their oppression, analyse it, and challenge it.

A woman who can name her oppression can fight it. That, I hope, is the legacy of The Second Sex."

Given what you have just said, Simone, would you define yourself as a political thinker?

"Not in the narrow meaning. I have been a politician or an activist in the traditional sense. But philosophy is never separate from politics. Ideas shape the world. Questioning the structures of existence is challenging for those who benefit from them.

The Second Sex is not a book about abstract thought but the reality of women's lives.

It reveals how personal struggles are tied to social oppression and how the most intimate experiences - love, marriage, and motherhood - are shaped by systems of power.

So, whether I intended it or not, I became a political thinker. Once you uncover an injustice, you cannot remain neutral. To ignore oppression is to be complicit in it."

Some say Sartre depended on you more than you depended on him. Would you agree?

"In some ways, yes. I am more practical and more stable. He leans on me for structure, for judgment, for clarity. I provide order to his chaos and precision to his thoughts.

But it's an exchange, which I don't mind. He gives me intellectual companionship, debate, and freedom in return.

Unlike the traditional muse, I did not exist to inspire him in silence. I challenge him and shape his ideas as much as he shapes mine.

If he depends on me, he recognises that I am an independent force, not an accessory to his work."

Finally, Simone, what advice would you give young feminists today?

"First, I would tell them: don't settle for mere inclusion. Don't fight only to be accepted into the existing order. Instead, reshape the world itself.

Second, people – mainly men- will tell you that progress so far is enough and that you should be grateful for the rights you have won.

But what good would sitting at the table be if the table was built to serve others? If the foundation remains unchanged, your seat is just another tool of control.

Third, do not be content with 'opportunities' that still require you to conform. Demand a world where you do not have to ask permission to exist on your own terms.

Finally, they will call you difficult, dangerous, or even radical. Let them.

Every woman who has changed history has been named the same. If they say you ask for too much, they fear what you will take."

THE MUSE PERSPECTIVE

Her impact as a muse extended far beyond Sartre. Claude Lanzmann, Violette Leduc, and Betty Friedan were some of the people most directly affected by her. Lanzmann, later known for his monumental film Shoah, absorbed de Beauvoir's relentless pursuit of truth.

A struggling writer, Leduc found literary confidence through de Beauvoir's encouragement, resulting in La Bâtarde, a raw and revolutionary autobiography.

Betty Friedan's The Feminine Mystique, often credited with launching second-wave feminism, was deeply influenced by The Second Sex, proving de Beauvoir's enduring influence on feminist thought.

The themes of freedom and autonomy ran through all aspects of her life. Her rejection of traditional relationships, particularly with Sartre, was not an affectation but a political stance.

She argued that love must be rooted in mutual freedom, not possession. This radical view challenged the very structure of love and inspired generations to rethink the connections between romance, autonomy, and gender.

De Beauvoir's influence extended beyond individuals to entire movements.

Feminism, philosophy, literature, and even modern existential thought bear the imprint of her defiance. She was not a muse who adorned the sidelines - she was the fire that forced others to think, write, and act.

Today, her work remains a cornerstone of feminist philosophy, proving that the most potent muses are those who do not merely inspire but challenge the world to change.

NOTE: Much has been written about de Beauvoir; you will be spoilt for choice. One of the most readable and well-researched accounts is Becoming Beauvoir by Kate Kirkpatrick, Bloomsbury Academic, 2020

TENNESSEE WILLIAMS

1906–1992

American playwright Tennessee Williams believed his works were profoundly shaped by his family relations with his father, mother, and sister.

Raised by a domineering father and an emotionally disturbed mother, this was a backdrop that profoundly influenced his creative journey.

Williams was deeply affected by muses, particularly women whose fragility, strength, and suffering reflected facets of his emotional terrain.

He, too, was a muse in his own right. Countless playwrights, actors, and writers found a raw, poetic truth in his work. They experienced him directly or indirectly as their muse.

With his indirect help, Method actors brought Williams's characters to life. Playwrights elsewhere sought to capture the same aching beauty of lost dreams that Williams shared through his work.

TENNESSEE WILLIAMS

It's late evening in 1978, and I'm about to meet Tennessee Williams in his private room at the Hotel Monteleone in New Orleans.

Maybe it is late, but Williams is a night owl, often finding inspiration and solace in the quiet hours.

He should feel at home here for our conversation since this is one of his favourite places. He even featured it in 'The Rose Tattoo', one of his most successful plays.

That atmosphere of faded grandeur, sensuality, and quiet melancholy lingers in many of his plays.

This spacious room, with views of the French Quarter, is ripe with classic furnishings reflecting the hotel's distinctive history.

Williams has spent his life here on and off. City sounds seep through the open window, and far-off strains of jazz music combine with the clip-clop of horse-drawn carriages.

On the desk, I see a well-used typewriter and scattered papers, suggesting his continuing creative work.

Predictably, an open bottle of bourbon rests on what might once have been a table, half-concealed by literary debris and glassware.

A clock in the background persistently ticks the hour. Williams enters as if working to a timetable.

He's wearing a silk dressing gown and holding a glass that appears to be more bourbon. And he offers me a welcoming smile with just a tinge of fatigue.

This renowned writer is sixty-seven, slightly scrawny and weather-beaten. On his face are lines from years of creative production and personal turmoil.

Still, he scans me with remarkable intelligence and intensity.

"You're the muse guy, right?"

Correct, Mr. Williams. I want to focus on the role of the muse. Can we begin with your childhood in Mississippi?

"Right back there, eh? OK. Mississippi has a way of getting under your skin. I was born in Columbus, a town in eastern Mississippi, near the Alabama border. It's not the romantic, sprawling locale that everyone thinks of.

My father, Cornelius, was a travelling shoe salesman - a brutal job, always on the road, a remote figure.

My mother, Edwina, was a Southern belle, or at least tried to be, with a hint of faded elegance.

In those early years, we never put down roots; we moved around a lot. That feeling of instability, of being an outsider, has stuck with me."

So, what was the atmosphere like in your childhood home?

Pouring from the bottle into his now-empty glass, he gestures for me to take some, but I decline.

"Sure. It was a mix of extremes. There was beauty, indeed. The lush scenery, the scent of magnolias, the leisurely pace of life. But tension simmered beneath the surface.

My father was, let's say, a man of his time and not always the most sensitive.

My mother, God love her, was bound by the ideals of Southern womanhood, but she was all nervous energy, fragile. And then there was Rose..."

Rose, your sister, did she shape the way you were raised?

"She was the centre of my world at home, my big sister. She was gentle, creative, and kind. We were inseparable.

But Rose was mentally troubled and a constant source of concern. It was an apparition haunting our family. I was drawn to her fragility and vulnerability. It informed my thoughts.

My sister became my muse, my confidant - and, ultimately, my tragedy. She had a hard life; she had a lobotomy, and she never really healed. That resonates with everything I've ever written."

What other things influenced you as a young mind?

"The constant moving and the feeling of being uprooted compounded this sense of dislocation. I was a shy, sensitive kid, not incredibly athletic, which didn't do me any favours among the other boys.

I wrote, and I read; I went to the library. It was a world of my own making, imagination, and escape.

Then there was the social order of the South, its strictures and unspoken codes.

Let me explain. This was a realm of appearances, where everything had to be kept hidden beneath a veneer of gentility.

That disconnect of hypocrisy between what people said and what they felt fascinated and repulsed me. It gave me a lot of material to work with."

Do you mean as a place to write about?

"No! The South is not only a place; it's a mindset. A country of contradictions, beauty and rot, tradition and repression. It clings to its past, even as it tries to move on.

The heat, humidity and oppression of life crawling slowly can wash over you with a sense of claustrophobia. And yet, something is charming and romantic about it, too.

It is brimming with storytellers, larger-than-life characters, and the deep stuff of humanity. It's in my blood. It comes back to me and to my work even if I think I have abandoned it."

And your literary influences?

Looking thoughtful and pouring more drink: "I love Chekhov for his subtlety, fear Poe's darkness, and have absorbed Faulkner's Southern Gothic richness.

I work hard to blend these elements into my distinctive theatrical voice. Audiences seem drawn to the resulting deep emotional resonance and poetic intensity.

However, many writers who find success will tell you that they struggle to write."

Do you think that holds for you, too?

"Yeah. For me, it's an inspiration and a torment. I write about things that haunt me that I can't escape from.

The syntax tumbles out like a fever dream. It hurts, but I have found it unavoidable.

I guess I have come to terms with it by now. It all amounts to a furiously energetic tango of inspiration and complete terror.

It's never a tidy process, not at all like clockwork. Sometimes, it's just one image, one snatch of conversation, one memory that ignites something in me, like a spark in dry tinder.

Or it's a slow, painful slog, wrestling with the words, fighting to articulate the shapeshifting emotions roiling inside me."

I begin to get the picture--seems your writing days must vary greatly.

"Yes, sometimes I write for days, surviving with barely any sleep. Other times, I sit staring at a blank page for hours, paralysed by self-doubt.

I usually write late at night when things are quiet and I hear my characters' whispers.

 I recall once working on Streetcar, and Blanche's situation left me reeling. I stayed up all night and wrote until dawn, sharing her desperation.

A *Streetcar Named Desire* was such a huge hit. Did you use specific rituals or habits to help you get the words on the page?

Laughing: "Coffee. Gallons of it. And cigarettes, of course. They have always been my faithful companions.

And music... I recall getting my fill of blues music while working on Cat on a Hot Tin Roof. It just felt so right with the characters' raw and visceral emotions.

And then there's the typewriter - an extension of my very self. The rat-a-tat of the keys is my constant soundtrack while I create.

If the keys aren't clacking, nothing's coming out - simple as that. No clacking means no output!"

Your plays are so varied in style, and I wonder where else you can find inspiration.

"Gee, that's a big one. I wish I knew for sure. I suppose if I did, I might not need to keep writing. But I can tell you this: I've never believed in strict realism.

Life isn't tidy, and neither are my plays. I try to write how memory feels, how longing aches, and how dreams flicker just out of reach. If I have one, a little poetry, pain, and madness, that's my style."

He sits back and takes a deep breath: "Life is a drama full of tragedy and comedy, love and loss. All you have to do is pay attention.

I recall being here in New Orleans, sitting in a bar, and overhearing a woman discussing her dreams and disappointments.

Her story and vulnerability stayed with me; it became the seed for a new play."

Yes, you are so prolific. I must ask: Do you often get writer's block?

"Are you kidding? It happens constantly. It's what writers call the curse. It's those days when the words don't hit the ground running, and it feels like you are headbutting a brick wall.

In those moments, I try to distance myself from work, go for a walk, listen to music, and do anything to clear my mind.

Sometimes, I even begin writing a different play, allowing my writing to continue. At times, the only cure is time. I just sit here waiting for inspiration to come back."

Perhaps we can return to the subject of muses. That's the main

reason I am bothering you, Tennessee. Do you consider yourself a muse?

"It's no bother. I'm enjoying your questions. They're getting my juices flowing.

A muse? It's a significant issue being able to stir something inside another person - an idea, a feeling, or a desperate need for something creative. I'm not sure if I'm that.

However, I am confident that my work benefits others. That includes writers, actors, and even everyday people who tell me about my plays and how they have made them look at themselves differently.

Maybe that's about as close as you get to being a muse, a voice that remains in someone's heart after the curtain falls."

Must a muse be a person, someone you actually meet?

"Not at all. A muse can be a person, but it can also be a place, a memory, or a feeling that won't leave you alone.

The South is my muse, with its heat, decay, and haunted beauty. My family, with all their tenderness and madness, is also my muse.

My sister, Rose, is perhaps my greatest muse when it comes to people. She's the most delicate thing I've ever known, and the world crushed her.

I write for her even though she's now permanently living in a care facility in St. Louis, Missouri. She exists in many of my characters, especially Laura Wingfield in The Glass Menagerie."

Have people told you that you've inspired them as well?

"Oh yes, and it humbles me every single time. There was the novelist and playwright Carson McCullers. She once said my writing 'touches *the heart like a blessing.*'

And young playwrights have come up to me, trembling and saying they saw The Glass Menagerie or A Streetcar Named Desire, and all at once, something inside of them unlocked.

Perhaps I let them be raw, and write with feeling, and let themselves ache on the page. If that's what a muse is, I'll gladly and gratefully wear the title."

Was there a particular moment when you realised that you had that impact on others?

"Yes. Once, a woman wrote to me after seeing The Glass Menagerie. She told me she had a daughter like Laura in the play, one who was painfully shy and lost in her own world.

She said that my play helped her better understand and love her daughter.

What more could a writer ask for? To be a mirror, a light, to give someone the words they didn't know they needed? That letter meant more to me than any review ever could."

"You've been widely quoted as saying: 'All great art is a confession'. Do you think that's part of what makes you a muse, that your writing permits others to confess their own truths?

"Absolutely. I believe that the artist's job is to take off the mask. To say, 'Here I am. Here is my longing, my fear, my madness.' When you dare to be utterly honest, you permit others to do the same.

And when you do that and are utterly honest, you permit others to do the same. I think that's why actors love my work.

People like Marlon Brando, Geraldine Page, and Kim Hunter. They've told me that my characters have allowed them to reach places within themselves they hadn't touched before.

And if I've helped others do that, then I suppose I've been a muse in my way."

Actors say my words feel different - not just lines to deliver, but places to live inside. They don't just speak their lines; they inhabit them."

Why do you think that is?

"Because I write with blood. I don't mean that literally, though some nights, it feels close to it! I write about real human frailty, about the things we try to hide from others and ourselves.

And that means actors don't just recite my words; they must embody them. They have to find the trembling, the breaking, the yearning underneath.

I once told Brando, 'Don't act Stanley, be Stanley.' And he did. That's the kind of art that stays with people. It lingers. It burns."

Do you think you've influenced playwrights in the same way?

"I hope so. I see echoes of my work in others; August Wilson, Tony Kushner, and even Arthur Miller have once admitted that I've helped push American theatre toward something more lyrical and poetic.

And young writers, too. Many say they've read A Streetcar Named Desire, and something inside them opened. I think that's the highest compliment I could get.

A true muse doesn't just spark one masterpiece - they set a lifetime of creation in motion. If my plays have done that, I am grateful."

You published your Memoirs three years ago. What led you to get it done at that point in your life's journey?

"I did it for reasons that were very personal to me. First, I thought I had to face my past and talk about my struggles with addiction, sexuality and mental health.

Biographers were always going to dissect them, so by writing my Memoirs, I took back some control of the narrative and shared my side of the story.

Another reason was that the Memoirs allowed me to reflect on my past successes and personal tragedies and demand to be taken seriously as someone who has impacted our culture.

When I wrote the book, I was still suffering over my partner Frank Merlo's death. So, as you'd expect, I filled the Memoirs with reflections on our relationship, and I guess it was a form of catharsis for my ongoing grief.

I also wanted to acknowledge what was then an open secret publicly: my homosexuality."

Yes, it was one of the first significant autobiographies by a literary figure, someone of your stature, to discuss homosexuality candidly.

Upending the Bourbon bottle into his now-empty glass, Williams swallows the amber liquid and shrugs, a half-smile flickering: 'I'm not done with the reasons.

Those Memoirs gave me a chance to confront my critics and candidly examine my failures.

I appreciate your honesty. My final question is this: If you could say one thing to a young writer starting, what would it be?

"Your muse lives inside you. It haunts you, in the places you can't forget, in the people you've loved and lost.

The key is to listen, be vulnerable, and let yourself feel deeply, even when it hurts, especially when it hurts the most."

THE MUSE PERSPECTIVE

This prolific artist was one of the most influential playwrights of the 20th century, famous for his intensely personal, poetic, and provocative works.

The most successful of these plays - A Streetcar Named Desire, The Glass Menagerie, and Cat on a Hot Tin Roof - revolve around themes of human fragility, desire, and the struggle for dignity.

Williams' legacy was cemented with multiple prizes: two Pulitzers, four New York Drama Critics' Circle Awards, and a Tony Award.

His work is still read and performed worldwide today, continuing to influence the course of modern drama.

Williams's impact stretched far beyond the stage and screen. His uncompromising examination of sex, mental illness and societal decay struck a chord with audiences around the world.

Consequently, it motivated writers, filmmakers and performers to push creative limits. His plays have become standard reference points in American and international theatre.

In Europe, directors such as Elia Kazan and Ingmar Bergman, in particular, staged his works to great acclaim.

The psychological complexity of his characters helped popularise Method Acting, with players like Marlon Brando and Vivian Leigh delivering career-defining performances.

Williams' legacy is visible in his plays and has seeped into numerous artistic movements and many lives. His poetic eye, his genius for compressing tensions of reality and illusion and his deeply human characters continue to inspire artists and writers.

NOTE: Tennessee Williams has been the subject of numerous biographies, reflecting his significant impact on American theatre and culture.

Among those currently available, a richly detailed and compelling read is Tennessee Williams: A Mad Pilgrimage of the Flesh by John Lahr (Bloomsbury, 2014), which won the National Book Critics Circle Award for Biography.

ALAN TURING

1912-1954

Turing is central to the history of modern computing. A pioneering mathematician, logician, and scientist, he aimed to create a theoretical machine that could compute any set of steps to solve a problem or complete a task.

It was the foundation of theoretical computer science.

As a respected mathematical scientist, Turing accepted the seemingly impossible assignment in World War II to break the impregnable German military Enigma code.

His iconic Turing Test remains a core element for assessing machine performance in comparison to human-like responses.

He created early computers and worked on ACE, one of the earliest stored-program computers. His insights have had a lasting impact on developmental biology, although much of his work went underappreciated during his lifetime.

ALAN TURING

"It is 1951, and I've come to Turing's quiet office hidden in one of Manchester University's older buildings, where he's a Reader in Mathematics.

It's a modest, functional space with shelves overflowing with academic detritus. The inevitable blackboard, covered in half-erased equations and logic diagrams, dominates one wall.

A tired-looking armchair sits brooding in the corner next to a small table bearing an empty teacup and a folded copy of The Manchester Guardian.

Apart from the occasional footsteps echoing in the corridor outside, I can only hear the quiet hum of an electric heater.

Manchester winters are harsh, and Turing - absentminded about everyday comfort - rarely thinks of warmth until the cold insists." Often absent-minded about practicalities, Turing seldom bothers with warmth until necessary.

One of Britain's greatest minds, Alan Turing, sits at his desk, spinning a pencil between his fingers.

He glances up, his expression neutral but assessing, before gesturing vaguely at the chair opposite him.

A discreet, padded folder I have brought with me today rests on the table between us. Without opening it, he offers a ghost of a smile, though it is hardly a vote of confidence: "All right, let's hear it, then."

I imagine you're wondering why I've asked to meet you in private, Dr. Turing.

"A little. I don't usually get to talk to outsiders much these days."

I have something here that might explain our meeting this morning. This folder is classified and only available to those with the appropriate clearance.

Turing stops spinning the pencil and picks up the file to study it. After flicking through it, he turns his gaze on me. "And what exactly does it say?"

I take back the folder from him and open it just enough to reveal a page detailing the work done at Bletchley Park. I explain:

As you can see, it includes the cryptographic breakthroughs at Hut 8 and your role, Dr. Turing, in breaking the Enigma cypher.

Turing straightens, his relaxed air giving way to alertness, his casual air slipping into something more guarded. He leans forward just slightly:

"That's a rather bold claim. Most of what we did there never made it past Whitehall."

Until recently. This official history was compiled for internal use. I'm not here to probe carelessly, Dr. Turing.

I understand the sensitivity. But I need you to know that I speak with knowledge, not speculation.

Turing leans back with arms crossed: "Let's test that, shall we?"

I read a key phrase aloud:

By mid-1940, Turing's development of the Bombe machine accelerated decryptions of Wehrmacht and Luftwaffe traffic, proving decisive in the Battle of the Atlantic.

Turing exhales suddenly while his expression remains unreadable. But his fingers visibly tighten against his arm: "You really have seen the files."

I wouldn't be here otherwise.

"Well then, you must be rather influential or very determined. You have my attention; what exactly do you wish to know?"

I'm here to discuss your unofficial role as a Muse and its considerable impact on others. Was there anyone who acted as a Muse for you?

Turing shrugs and frowns: "I'm not sure about a single source. However, I grew up with numbers, which always made more sense to me than people.

But Christopher Morcom, whom I met at Sherborne school, had an extraordinary mind and great intellectual curiosity, which I found intensely stimulating. Chris's work was always better than mine because he was very thorough.

He had remarkable powers in discovering the most effective way to do anything.

He could estimate when a minute had passed to within half a second. His early death was terrible, and I lost my closest intellectual companion. As I wrote to his mother, '*I worshipped the ground; he walked on.*'

His death became the engine behind my pursuit of mathematics and logic. The loss drove me to pursue them even more intensely.

These shaped my thoughts on consciousness, artificial intelligence, and even the nature of the soul.

You see, Christopher was not just a friend but a Muse, a force that compelled me toward relentless inquiry, the pursuit of deep questions about intelligence and computing."

Apart from Christopher, did specific teachers or mentors act as an intellectual stimulus to you?"

"Yes, the mathematics teacher at Sherborne recognised my potential. He encouraged me when others dismissed my unconventional thinking.

At Sherborne, I chose to ignore Latin and Greek, instead focusing on relativity and quantum mechanics.

Do you know that I was once caught doing algebra during a divinity lesson? Anyway, my studying approach won no praise from most of my teachers, but the reactions made me more resilient.

The more they dismissed my methods, the more I saw the need to forge my way.

Sherborne taught me that institutions resist change, but it doesn't mean that change is impossible. I learned to work around the system rather than against it."

May we now proceed to your time at Cambridge in the 1930s? How did this affect you?

In many ways, Cambridge was a revelation, both intellectually and personally.

In 1932, my reading of the new work by the mathematician, physicist, computer scientist, and engineer von Neumann significantly altered my thinking.

His logical foundations of quantum mechanics helped me move from emotional to rigorous intellectual enquiry."

And personally?

"Cambridge was the first place I felt I could breathe more freely, even if I still needed to be careful.

The atmosphere was more tolerant than I had known before. There were others like me, some open, some discreet. That knowledge alone was liberating.

Self-acceptance, though, didn't happen all at once. I was still deciphering myself, so to speak.

There was no grand epiphany, no moment of revelation, just a gradual awareness. The feelings had always been there.

At Sherborne, I had these feelings for Christopher Morcom, though I would only later understand what they truly meant.

At Cambridge, they deepened and became more specific. But certainty is not the same as ease. I knew the law. I knew the risks. And yet, I also knew that this was how I was.

And what does one do with the inescapable truth of oneself? One lives with it. One calculates the risks, like any good mathematician, but one does not deny the equation itself."

You mentioned earlier how your reactions to others at school made you more resilient. Can you think of a later time when you really needed this part of your personality?

"I certainly can. During the war, Prime Minister Winston Churchill visited Bletchley.

He was impressed by my team's work on coding. After such a prestigious call, we assumed we'd get some of the needed supplies. We waited and waited.

That's when resilience was absolutely needed. My team and I

bypassed our boss, who had tried and failed to obtain the supplies.

We wrote a joint letter to Churchill and had it hand-delivered to his office. We begged him to sort out our supply problem and explained in stark terms why it was so critical.

He acted right away. Again, it didn't make me popular, but we got what we needed."

In your 1936 paper on computable numbers, you explained that meant "a machine able to write down its decimal." Was it a muse that stimulated the development of this abstract idea, which became the Turing Machine?

"Sometimes I wonder about that myself. My Muse, if you call it that, took the form of a problem: how can a machine determine the truth of mathematical statements?

That's when the idea of an abstract machine, a thinking machine, took hold.

So, you see, the inspiration was not a person but the boundless potential of logic itself.

Initially, it was theoretical, but I quickly saw its potential. If a machine can somehow compute anything that can be expressed mathematically, there are enormous implications.

At Bletchley Park, the challenge of using such knowledge to crack the Enigma puzzle, which involved breaking the German coding machine, felt overwhelming.

One of the most serious difficulties was not letting the enemy know our victories over them were due to code-breaking work."

How did you become involved with Bletchley, England's most

secret and mysterious place?

"It's probably in this file here. But in 1938, I'd just returned from my study year in the US, and my King's fellowship had been renewed. I knew the authorities were seeking people to help with decoding work.

Out of interest, I took a cryptology course at the Government Code and Cypher School. You can guess the rest.

At Bletchley, we needed help to reduce the tedium and complexity of constant code-breaking work.

That's when we developed the Bombe - a machine built to break the unbreakable. My inspiration for it wasn't a person or a mystical Muse.

It stemmed from patterns found in logic, numbers and behaviour.

The enemy's behaviour using the Enigma machine meant that cracking it was not just about brute force of numbers. It also involved understanding how the enemy thought."

During all that time, you also had the strain of resolving your personal life, didn't you?

"What a question! Secrecy in one's personal life, let alone in the professional sphere, exacts a terrible toll. It forces one to construct walls, even in thought.

Yes, I found it challenging to come to terms with my feelings. But I would prefer not to talk more about that now."

I understand. Let's discuss your recent election as a Fellow of the Royal Society. Are your ideas in computing finally being recognised?

"Naturally, it's an honour to be elected. I'm more interested in what thinking machines will achieve in the years ahead.

My work on computability and machine intelligence almost certainly earned this distinction.

It's gratifying, but I doubt my colleagues fully grasp what lies ahead - or how these ideas may reshape society."

Your work has had a profound influence on many of your contemporaries. Who do you feel has been most affected by it?

"That's not easy to say for sure. However, the brilliant mathematician and physicist John von Neumann built on the ideas of computability that I explored in my early papers.

For example, his work on stored programs is already shaping the next generation of machines. It will be fascinating to see theory becoming practice."

Donald Knuth, the renowned computer scientist, also cites you as an essential influence on his work in algorithms and programming.

"Donald? He's still relatively young, but I believe he has a brilliant mind. If my work has contributed to his thinking, that's gratifying, though the ideas of computation belong to no one person.

What I proposed was simple: a formal way of describing what a machine could, in theory, accomplish."

That leads me to ask about your recent paper, *Computing Machinery and Intelligence*, where you proposed the "Imitation Game," now known as the "Turing Test. How did you come up with this idea?

"I ignored debates about whether machines 'truly' think and instead asked: if a machine's behaviour is indistinguishable from a human's, shouldn't we call it intelligent?

I suspect this question will spark debate for decades to come.

Let's first assume sufficient complexity and the ability to learn from experience.

With enough time and effort, I see no fundamental reason why machines could not exhibit intelligence comparable to ours."

That is indeed a fascinating thought. But going back to your wartime work, where is it leading now?

"The principles we developed, such as statistical analysis, pattern recognition, and automation, are fast becoming fundamental in many fields, not just cryptography.

The war taught us that problems once considered insurmountable can be tackled systematically. That lesson is applicable far beyond codes and cyphers."

How do you think people in the future will engage with your arguments about machine intelligence?

"I suspect the notion of a machine that can think or convincingly imitate thinking will trouble them greatly.

As machines become increasingly complex, so too will the ethical, intellectual, and emotional questions we must confront.

The more they delve into the intricacies of machine learning, the more issues they will encounter that need resolving.

Frankly, I wish them luck!"

THE MUSE PERSPECTIVE

Alan Turing demonstrated how the Muse sometimes has a role far beyond that of a single individual.

He inspired contemporaries and thinkers, creators and activists across disciplines and generations.

His influence is felt not only through technology but also in literature, film, philosophy, and social justice movements.

Turing's theoretical insights lit the fuse of the digital revolution. His concept of the Universal Machine laid the foundation for computer science.

His wartime service at Bletchley Park was one of the most impressive intellectual achievements of the 20th century.

Tim Berners-Lee, the inventor of the World Wide Web, has said that Turing's work is fundamental to the digital universe in which we live now.

But Turing's legacy extends far beyond mathematics and computation.

His persecution due to his homosexuality, tragic death, and posthumous pardon have made him a significant symbol in the global struggle for LGBTQ+ rights.

Turing and his life are both a warning and a beacon of genius, injustice, and enduring legacy.

Writers and artists, too, have found Turing a captivating Muse. His story has been brought to life in books, stage plays, and film, making the world more aware of his genius and struggles.

Turing's visionary thinking and influence were decades ahead of his time. He remains an eternal Muse for those who dare to think beyond the possible.

NOTE: Numerous biographies and papers about Turing's life exist. Some are comprehensive yet suffer from excessive detail and poor writing.

Perhaps the most readable and accessible is Alan Turing by Dermot Turing, a relative of his, published by History Press in 2021.

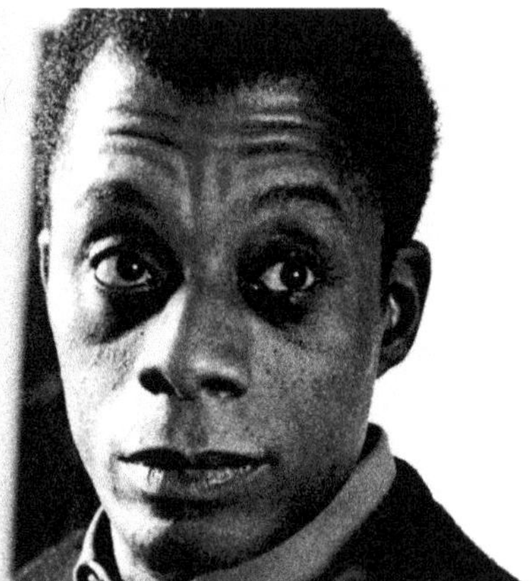

JAMES BALDWIN

1924–1987

James Baldwin is one of the most potent and essential voices of the 20th century. As a young man, he fled to Paris from America in the late 1940s.

As a writer, Baldwin would never look away from injustice. His works, from Go Tell It on the Mountain to The Fire Next Time, explored race, identity, sexuality, and the human condition with unparalleled depth and honesty.

He stood at the crossroads of the civil rights movement. He conversed with figures like Martin Luther King Jr. and Malcolm X while mentoring younger generations of writers and activists.

Whether through his literature or his impassioned speeches, Baldwin's influence extended far beyond the written page.

Today, he remains a model for those who seek truth, justice, and the courage to speak boldly.

JAMES BALDWIN

There is a delightful view over the quiet hilltop of Saint-Paul-de-Vence in France. Dusk creeps slowly into our presence while the sky deepens into amber, washing the stone streets in a soft glow.

On an evening in 1980, I am visiting James Baldwin, a prolific American writer now living most of the time in this pleasant house on the edge of the village.

Candles flicker against the walls, their light dancing over a current manuscript-in-progress. His hair, now flecked with grey, is cropped close.

His hands are elegant but calloused from decades of writing. His white linen shirt is unbuttoned at the collar, sleeves rolled up, an effortless elegance that suits his presence. A glass of cognac rests within reach.

There is no rush to his words, no impatience, only the measured rhythm of a man who has spent his life thinking deeply, challenging the world with his voice and an inseparable typewriter.

After a few moments, he gestures to a leather chair by the open window. "Ok, now you're here, what can I do for you?"

Mr Baldwin, thank you for agreeing to spend some time with me.

"Please just call me James or Jimmy; I'd feel more comfortable with that.

Anyway, I imagine you didn't come all this way for small talk," he says with a slight grin. So, what do you really want to know?"

My primary mission is to discuss your role as a Muse.

But let's start with your first book in 1953, _Go Tell It on the_

Mountain. **Reflecting on those early days, why do you think this first attempt was important?**

"That's a fair question, and I have often wondered about it, maybe because it touched on themes of religion, race, identity, and personal struggle.

I tried to share the trauma of Black existence in America, generational pain, and the oppressive weight of religion in the lives of Black families."

This was both deeply personal and yet reflected the reality for many Black families.

"Yes, I was inspired by my own experiences of growing up in Harlem, my journey of self-discovery, faith, and dealing with racial oppression.

I enjoyed weaving my struggles into the broader universal human experience. I wanted it to be more than just a story of a Black boy in Harlem, but an exploration of issues such as identity, faith, and power, regardless of race or culture.

Your fearlessness about racial injustice and the book's deeply personal themes of sexuality and identity made you a Muse for generations of writers, activists, and thinkers.

"You're kind to say so. But I agree that the book laid a good foundation for further writing.

Success gave me the courage to be an even more direct critic of American racism, a human rights defender, and to encourage other artists and activists."

Well, you've inspired so many people, James. Some have described you as a Muse. Do you see yourself that way?

Baldwin laughs softly, "A Muse? That's a fancy word for what I do. I've never thought of myself as anyone's Muse. I'm merely trying to bear witness, to name what I see and feel.

I'm grateful if I have managed to light a fire in others. But I never set out to inspire. In the early days, at least, I was trying to survive."

But you have lit fires in people, James. Writers like Toni Morrison, for example. She's acknowledged that your work helped open doors for her.

"Toni saw what it meant to be a Black writer who tells the truth and refuses to be quiet. She walked that road, too.

If I were a giant to her, it was only because we were part of the same struggle. But she needed no Muse; she would always be brilliant.

If I played a role, it was in reminding her - and every Black writer - that our stories matter. That we belong on the page, in our full complexity."

And Maya Angelou? She has said that you were the one who encouraged her to write I Know Why the Caged Bird Sings.

"Yes, she didn't think she could write her story, but I knew she could. The way she carried herself and spoke, she was already writing, just not on paper yet. All I gave her was a little nudge. She would have done it anyway."

Beyond literature, your influence can also be felt in music. Take Nina Simone, for example.

He laughs, shaking his head: "Nina is like my sister. She sings about revolution. Her words shape movements, give language to ignored struggles, and light a path for generations to follow.

She and I can argue one minute and embrace the next. She doesn't just sing; she wages war with her voice."

Younger voices are beginning to emerge. And whether they realise it or not, filmmakers who use their art to challenge the world are also starting to see you as a literary ancestor.

"It is kind of you to say so. I hope I have helped clear a path for black writers and activists to explore sexuality, identity, and truth, without apology. When I wrote Giovanni's Room in 1956, they didn't just hate the book - they feared what it revealed. Some called me a traitor and said I was airing dirty laundry."

Yes, you wrote about homosexuality, bi-sexuality, and straight relationships. It remains a heady mixture for a novel.

"Oh, how they hated me for that book. The Americans said I had betrayed my race by writing about white men.

The French just called it "tragic" and moved on. And the Black community, well, many of them preferred not to talk about it at all.

But love is love, no matter what the world says. I am proud that young writers can speak openly about who they are today. That means something.

Those young men, such brave souls. They are saying things that I did not say. They tell the truth in ways the world is even less ready to hear. They fight so that Black writers and activists can explore sexuality and identity without apology.

And that fills me with hope because I've spent so much of my life knowing that people like us have always existed, but we've been written out of history."

Another person you deeply affected was Audre Lorde. She read

your work early on and, in some ways, followed your path - writing about race, sexuality, and identity with fierce honesty.

"Ah, Audre. Now, there's a woman who doesn't just walk through fire - she dances in it, shapes it, makes it her own. She doesn't need me to give her courage. She was born with it.

But if my work has done anything, perhaps it showed Audre that a Black writer can tell the truth and still stand. Audre is fierce - because she must be.

She knows what the world asks of Black women, the weight of both race and gender pressing on their backs. And she does not bow. She speaks. She fights. She insists on being heard."

Given all these examples of your influence, do you still reject the idea of being a Muse?

Pausing to light a cigarette: "I see myself as a witness. A witness to my people, my time, and the human heart. If that makes me a Muse, then I won't argue.

But I never wanted people to look at me that way. I wanted them to look at themselves. Maybe that's what a Muse really does, after all."

Given the ground we've covered, James, and if it's not a crass question now, could you please explain how you got here?

What about your childhood? How did childhood in Harlem shape your path towards writing?

"Harlem's still with me - always will be. It wasn't just where I grew up; it was the furnace where I was forged.

Harlem did not just teach me to struggle; it gave me my music, language, and rhythm and put the heartbeat in my prose. The voices on the street, the cadence of a sermon in the church, and the defiant laughter in the face of hardship all became the foundation of my writing.

Yes, Harlem gave me pain, but it also gave me poetry. Without it, I would not exist as a writer."

What about your preaching experience as a teenager? Does that still shape your speech and writing?

"Of course. The pulpit teaches you the power of the voice. When I preached, I had to make people feel something, stir them, and move them to action. That is the same demand placed on the writer.

The church gave me language and rhythm, but it also gave me something to rebel against.

I saw how religion could be used to control people, to make them fearful. Leaving the church was necessary, but it never really left me. It remains in the cadence of my words."

You didn't just leave the church, Jimmy; you abandoned America for Paris. Why was that?

"At the time, I was struggling financially and emotionally, living in New York, and a close friend had committed suicide. I hadn't yet published a book, and my primary goal in leaving was survival, not literary success.

I also wanted more creative freedom. Life in America was suffocating; I faced immense racism and doubted my ability to survive the fury of the colour problem there.

Paris, with its vibrant community of expatriate artists and intellectuals, offered me a sense of distance and creative possibilities.

I must mention that I was broke when I arrived there and lived in poverty, taking odd jobs and sometimes sleeping in cafés.

Thankfully, Richard Wright helped me get a fellowship to support my writing. I appreciate what he did for me, but we later fell out when I critiqued his writing.

I loved Paris, but I could never settle there permanently. I have moved frequently between France, Turkey, and the US.

In America, I was always a Negro first, a writer second. In Paris, I was simply a man. It did not mean I was free of America; America was always in me.

But I could finally look at it from a distance, dissect it, understand it."

In looking at things from a distance, James, what do people misunderstand most about you?

"They don't realise that I'm always writing about love. Even when I write about anger, race, or power, I am writing about love. Because love is the only real revolution."

THE MUSE PERSPECTIVE

James Baldwin was a writer who fully witnessed the complexities of race, love, human suffering, and the world's stubborn refusal to reckon with its injustices.

His works are profoundly individual, yet they are also universally applicable.

They are for those who have ever searched for their place in the world, for anyone who has been made invisible, and for everyone who can't be silenced.

James Baldwin did not ask to be a Muse. He bore witness. And that act - naming, confronting, refusing silence - was the most powerful inspiration.

As an unconventional kind of Muse, he was not a quiet voice. Instead, he was energy, a storm, a truth that could not be ignored. His words inspired writers and activists.

But Baldwin was never simply an American or a Black writer; he was a writer of the human soul.

His words are those of many who have suffered exclusion and strive to change the world, to comprehend the beauty and agony of existence.

He did not demand admiration or seek to be anyone's Muse. And yet, he became one, not because he wished to inspire but because he told the truth so entirely that others could not help but be moved by it.

His legacy is not statues or monuments. He lit the fire in the hearts of those who came after him.

NOTE: An account of Baldwin's life you may find enjoyable: James Campbell, Talking at the Gates: A Life of James Baldwin, Paperback, Polygon, 2021.

MAYA ANGELOU

1928-2014

The air around Maya Angelou crackled with power. To speak with her was to be wrapped in wisdom, humour, and a rock-solid belief in the power of words.

She dedicated her life to creating art and making a difference. Her poetry and prose have nourished generations, shepherding the lost, the fragile, and the marginalised.

Maya Angelou was a true Muse, a thought-provoker, the flame of courage, and the mother of forbidden words.

This human dynamo cannot be pigeonholed. She was an actor, singer, playwright, journalist, screenwriter, poet, teacher, honorary university professor, activist, and in-demand speaker.

With her myriad talents and interests, she was often described as a Renaissance woman - a fitting description for someone who had a hand in many aspects of the arts and society.

MAYA ANGELOU

She's statuesque, wearing a long black dress, her head held high, a pair of gold earrings catching the low light.

It is the mid-1990s, and she greets me with a knowing smile. Her voice is rich and steady.

We are in the New York Schomburg Centre for Research in Black Culture in Harlem, which rings with history.

Its walls are filled with various images, and Maya Angelou stands before them as if waiting to join them.

Having spotted me, she waves lightly towards the next-door reading room: "Hey, welcome. Let's go in here; we have much to discuss."

As we find a quiet corner, I return her warm greeting: **"Maya Angelou, I'm so happy you could find the time to talk." Thanks for sparing the time.**

"Glad to help with your project, which I understand is about Muses, correct?"

Sure, but first, I want to know about your earliest memories of storytelling and poetry. How did these shape your view of the world?

"Let's see. My grandmother had a store in Stamps, Arkansas, where I learned what listening means.

The men who walked into the store spoke with thick Southern accents, their week's wages in hand, and the women told their stories through whispers and laughter.

As a child, I understood that these stories were sacred and grasped the power of words.

And I experienced something traumatic, which I would rather not discuss now. It caused me to stop speaking when I was eight, and for almost five years, I was mute."

So, silence became a powerful aspect of your childhood. What changed, and how did it transform into your most potent tool, language?

"I met a family friend, a well-respected woman in our black community called Mrs. Bertha Flowers. She played a pivotal role in helping me regain my voice.

She took me under her wing. She introduced me to poetry and literature, mainly works by Shakespeare, black poets like Paul Laurence Dunbar, and classics like A Tale of Two Cities.

She paid special attention to the spoken word, encouraging me to read poetry aloud and appreciate its rhythm and beauty.

Most importantly, I learned that words also have the power to heal, and I rediscovered my voice.

Silence taught me to listen, and listening trained me to understand.

That is why, when I speak, I do not throw words away. I place them carefully, knowing they will land where they're needed.

From the moment I found my voice, I knew I was responsible for those who came before me and those who had yet to arrive. Every poem, every speech, every moment on stage was a brushstroke on a larger canvas.

I chose words that would outlive me, stories that could be carried forward. I have spoken in a way that reaches the ears and the bones because it lingers across lifetimes.

When I break my silence, I do not speak softly. Instead, I speak with the fullness of all that had been kept inside me."

Could you briefly discuss your family life, particularly your son, Guy?

"Oh, my family life - it's a trip. My childhood was marked by instability, mainly in the aftermath of my parents' separation. My brother, Bailey, and I moved to live with our grandmother in Stamps, Arkansas.

Those formative years were filled with both hardship and love. My strict grandmother was a massive influence.

She showed me how to walk with my head held high in the face of the ugliness of racism that was all around us.

Then everything changed when Guy was born in 1944. Motherhood was one of the most life-altering experiences.

Guy gave me a purpose, a reason to fight for a better world for him and others.

Our relationship was sacred, and I was fiercely protective of him. I didn't want him to go through the same pain and struggle I did.

Having a child, though, also made me reflect deeply on the world I was living in. The world needed change, and I channelled that change into my work.

Writing about our stories - particularly those of Black women - became a form of protection for my son, myself, and the next generation.

My love for Guy helped fuel my activism and creativity, and I always wanted him to see that we had the power to rise no matter how difficult things became.

As for our relationship, well, it hasn't been very easy. Guy

Raising Guy often took precedence over everything else in my life. And though I've had wonderful friends and partners along the way, my focus was always on raising him to be strong, thoughtful, and compassionate.

I wanted him to see a world full of possibilities, even when it seemed bleak."

Thank you for being so frank about Guy and your family. Your role as a Muse is of particular interest to me today, Maya, if I may call you that.

"Yes, of course, call me Maya; it is not just a name; I cherish it for its vibrancy."

I understand and agree. Perhaps you could elaborate on how you became Maya Angelou and how that influenced your impact on others.

"My name! Well, that's a story in itself. I was born Marguerite Ann Johnson, but the name 'Maya' came from my brother, Bailey.

When we were young, he couldn't quite pronounce my name, and he started calling me 'Mya,' which eventually morphed into 'Maya.' It stuck, and from then on, everyone called me that.

I took 'Angelou' later, after starting my performing career. It was my new reinvention, embracing the next chapter in my life. It has a particular sound to it - one that is graceful.

I wanted a name that represented my transformation, my wings toward a life of purpose and expression. 'Angelou' also relates to 'angel,' a word which, in my opinion, signifies hope, strength and the will to rise above.

My name has shaped how I view myself and the world. It's almost a marker for the journey I've taken, from a little girl trying to make sense of trauma and loss to a woman who is claiming her power and her voice.

My name is the freedom to become different and rise above who people thought I could be. It reminds us that even something as simple as a name can have profound effects and meaning.

And, yes, my name has had an impact on my work. Evolution and constant reinvention are deeply tied to my writing, activism, and how I voice and express myself.

Ultimately, the name "Maya Angelou" transcended its original meaning. It became my identity, life's work, and contribution to the world."

Could you tell me a bit about your acting work? For example, in your youth, you went on tour.

"I was in my twenties, and the experience was my passport to the world. I wanted experience, culture, and the chance to stretch beyond the borders I was born into.

Singing in Porgy and Bess took me to Italy, Yugoslavia, Egypt, and beyond. Imagine a young Black woman from St. Louis performing in opera houses across Europe and Africa.

It was liberation dressed as music.

But it was more than a performance. It was witnessing how art can build bridges and how audiences responded to the soul of the music, even when they didn't share the language.

And it taught me discipline: rehearsals, stagecraft, and the nuance of voice.

Later, I drew on all that when I began writing seriously. Rhythm, breath, and timing exist in poetry as much as in song."

You are known for your poetry, Maya. Does it have the ability to change lives as profoundly as music or politics?

"Without a doubt! Poetry is the rhythm of the soul. The first music we hear is our mothers' lullabies and our grandmothers' humming.

This experience moves us before we understand it, and that is where its power lies. It does not have to be convincing; it simply is. Poetry, my dear, is the heart of change."

You're known to have inspired so many. What made you want to nurture their voices?

"Oprah is a woman who listens with her whole body. She absorbs wisdom and reshapes it into something the world needs.

She has always had the gift of asking the right questions, reaching into the depths of another's story, and holding it carefully.

Common is a poet who walks with rhythm in his soul. His music carries truth, and when spoken with clarity, truth will always resonate.

When I first spoke with him, I knew he had the heart of a Griot, the West African storyteller, historian, poet, and musician. A Griot keeps the oral tradition and carries a people's history.

Common preserves history, inspires social change, and connects generations through his words.

And then there's Toni Morrison. We've walked the same road in different ways.

She understands the necessity of telling our stories, of ensuring that our voices do not disappear into the background of history.

She wrote our people into existence on the literary stage and is one of those who carry the flame and pass it on."

Your poem *Still I Rise* has inspired activists, artists, and musicians and fueled movements. What do you think gives it such enduring power?

"Ah, my dear, that is the beauty of the word. A word well-placed, a phrase well-hewn, can travel farther than the feet that carried it and sink deeper than the soul that first gave it breath.

Still, I Rise was born from knowing. Knowing that the spirit rises no matter how the world presses its weight upon us, no matter how often it tries to silence or bend us. It must rise."

It's become an anthem. We've seen it chanted in protests, woven into music, and even referenced by hip-hop artists like Tupac and Common.

"Oh, Tupac! That young man has a passion, a poet's fire, wrapped in defiance. When I wrote Still I Rise, I, too, wrote about defiance.

I wrote for the ancestral voices that sang in the fields, for the labourers who built nations with hands calloused by injustice.

I was writing for the dreamers, activists, and the young girl who looks in the mirror and wonders if she is enough.

I know my poem has done its work when I hear my words echo in song, marches, and whispered affirmations before a courtroom battle. It has stepped beyond me."

You wrote it with history in mind, but it remains as powerful today. What do you think it is about the poem that speaks to so many generations?

"It is because oppression, my dear, is a shape-shifter. It changes its clothing, but its intent remains to stifle and diminish. But resilience, too, has an intent. So, too, does the rising.

There is a rhythm in Still I Rise - a pulse, a sway. It is defiant but joyous, unyielding but graceful.

Whether in 1978 or here and now, it reminds the reader that survival is about enduring and thriving, rising with laughter, dance, and unshaken dignity."

Some people say it gives them courage when they feel beaten down.

"Yes, because it is a promise. A summoning. A refusal to be swallowed by despair. Think of all the women who have whispered it to themselves before walking into rooms that tried to unsee them.

Or think of the young men who have turned to it when the world told them they were less than. For them, I wrote:

You may trod me in the very dirt,

But still, like dust, I'll rise.

 - Still I Rise

It reminds us that nothing can dampen the human spirit, not a cruel word, a bent law, or even a dire history."

What do you think a Muse does differently than a teacher or mentor?

"A Muse beckons, a mentor teaches, a teacher builds the stage. A teacher says, 'Now this is a lesson; learn this well. A mentor might respond, *'I'll show you how it's done.'*

But a Muse? A Muse sparks something that already lives within. A Muse doesn't tutor or enlighten; she reminds and rouses.

The correct word, the right note, the right moment of truth, and just like that, the soul remembers what it always knew."

If you could sit down with one historical figure who was a Muse for you, perhaps a writer, activist, or musician, who would it be, and what would you ask them?

"It would be Frederick Douglass, the most important movement leader for African American civil rights in the 19th century.

After escaping from slavery in Maryland, Douglass emerged as a national leader in the abolitionist movement, particularly in Massachusetts and New York.

During this time, he gained fame for his powerful oratory and incisive antislavery writings.

I would sit at his feet and ask, *'How did you do it?'* How did a man born in chains shape words so powerful they broke those very chains?

How do you carry both rage and hope in equal measure? How do you see a future of freedom while standing in the depths of oppression?

I would ask if he ever doubted that his words would reach us, that we would still be listening. And then I would tell him, we are. We are still listening."

As a Muse who has affected many people, what do you hope will be your legacy?

"Legacy is not an accidental afterthought; it is an intention. A Muse is not tethered to time. A Muse does not age.

What moves a woman's heart in 1925 can move a girl's heart one hundred years later if that Muse speaks the truth.

To be a Muse who leaves a worthwhile legacy, one must embody something eternal: courage, love, resilience, and justice.

When Toni Morrison found something in my words, and Oprah carried them forward, and when young poets shape their voices in response, it is not to me that they are responding; it is the enduring human experience.

The artist may pass, but the Muse lingers in the echoes."

Finally, Maya, what advice would you give those who wish to inspire others and want to be a Muse like you have been?

"Be courageous. If you are too afraid to live your truth, create what you want to be, and show up, what right do you have to try to inspire anyone else?

No matter where you are, what has been done to you, or who has tried to silence you, you must have something that cannot be put down."

Maya relaxes slightly in her chair, the low light gleaming off her gold earrings once again. Then she finishes, after a beat, "And don't ever shrink yourself down for someone else's comfort." Your voice matters."

As the evening dims and Maya's words linger in the air, it's clear her legacy is not a moment - it's a movement.

THE MUSE PERSPECTIVE

Maya Angelou was the essence of being a Muse, a lasting source of endurance, direction and awakening.

Her words and presence gave hope to generations, enabling them to reclaim their voices, particularly those who had been historically silenced.

Her autobiographical writings, beginning with I Know Why the Caged Bird Sings, offered her testimony and a mirror for readers seeking dignity, resilience, and truth.

A terrific poet, Angelou wrote poems such as Still I Rise that were a call to arms for the downtrodden.

Her poetry wove personal strength with collective struggle, offering rhythms of survival and defiance that transcended borders.

Her literal and literary voice reached millions, culminating in her historic recitation of "On the Pulse of Morning" at President Clinton's 1993 inauguration.

Angelou, the person, was a powerhouse of the civil rights movement, working on the front lines alongside Martin Luther King Jr. and Malcolm X.

Her activism was not limited to protests, but was woven into her art, teaching, and diplomacy.

As an ambassador and educator, she served as a bridge between cultures, advocating for African American arts and global solidarity. Her legacy is enormous.

NOTE: Apart from *her own writings*, you may enjoy *Maya Angelou: A Glorious Celebration* by Marcia Ann Gillespie et al. Bantam Doubleday, April 2008.

PRINCE

1928-2014

The musician Eric Clapton was once asked, 'What's it like being the best guitarist in the world?' He famously replied, 'I don't know - ask Prince!'

Few artists have fused genius and mystery quite like Prince. With total command of sound, style, and spectacle, he wasn't just a performer - he was a force. Part mystic, part rebel, constantly evolving, Prince didn't just make music - he lived it.

Able to play more than twenty instruments, he wrote, produced, and recorded with rare independence, crafting a sound all his own - a bold mix of punk, rock, R&B, and pop.

In this rare and imaginary exchange, he speaks about what it means to inspire, provoke, and guide others by being unapologetically oneself.

PRINCE

In a velvet suit, ruffled shirt, heels clicking like punctuation marks on marble, Prince walks into the room as if it belongs to him - because it does.

It's 1987, and Paisley Park gleams like a dream made solid: part sanctuary, part spaceship. The air is charged. This architectural concoction is where Prince creates worlds.

I'm here to discuss inspiration with the artist. About being a Muse. But even with my questions ready, something about Prince - his intensity, his stillness - makes me hesitate. He notices.

"Nice to meet you," he says, "I've got half an hour before a shoot. What's on your mind?"

Thanks for making time to meet. You've accomplished so much already. How do you turn that much creativity into focus?

"You have to shut the world out. Let the music find you. One day, it's funk. Another day, it's a whisper in jazz. Sometimes, it's just a feeling that won't leave you alone."

He sweeps his hand across the room. "This? This is where I get free, and the rules can't follow."

So, how did you start out? For instance, how did your upbringing shape that need to make music?

"My father played piano, jazz deep in his fingers. Mom could sing the pain of a note. That house was full of sound - Louisiana soul and Minneapolis chill.

I was breathing rhythm before I had words. Music wasn't something I chose. It chose me."

And your name - Prince? Where did that come from?

"That was my father's stage name - Prince Rogers. He wanted me to have no ceiling. Told a journalist once he named me so I could 'do everything I wanted to do.'

But I didn't feel like a Prince. I asked folks to call me Skipper. It took me time to grow into it."

You were born epileptic, right?

"Yeah. I had seizures as a kid. Scared the whole family - and me too. One night, I told my mom, *'I'm not gonna be sick no more.'* She said, 'Why?' I said, *'Because an angel told me.'* And just like that, they stopped.

You learn early that the world bends when you believe hard enough."

You seemed to find success early - your first album went platinum at 18 - but you also loved stirring things up.

"Yes, controversy makes people look twice. I like that. My album Controversy came out in '81. Played with the Stones that year. Opened in a trench coat and bikini briefs.

Got booed and pelted with trash. Didn't matter. Made 'em feel something."

Why build Paisley Park here, in Minnesota?

"Space. Freedom. 65,000 square feet of don't-tell-me-what-to-do.

I grew up in Minneapolis and never saw a place that allowed artists to be fully themselves, so I created one.

I wanted a studio, a concert hall, a rehearsal space, and a place to dream, all under one roof. There would be no need to fly to L.A. or bow to industry pressure. Middlemen? They dilute the current.

Here, I answer only to the music. Everything in this building - from the acoustics to the architecture - was designed to protect the vibe."

The Controversy album pushed boundaries after your previous one, *Dirty Mind*, and the song that went with it. What made it work?

"It had a pulse. Funk, rock, new wave - tight grooves with sharp edges. It was sharper than anything I'd done before. There was tension in those tracks, tension that matched the world outside.

I wasn't trying to be safe - I was trying to wake people up. It pushed buttons on purpose, and people felt that. It wasn't just sound. It was a statement."

Your fashion broke the rules, too. Masculine and feminine, blended boldly.

"Why live in a box? Gender and style are tools, not cages. I wore lace, heels, crop tops, and eyeliner - not to shock, but to express. Clothes are like chords. Mix them right; they sing. In the '80s, that freaked some people out.

Good. Art should wake you up. Sign o' the Times wasn't decoration. AIDS, addiction, poverty - I wasn't gonna look away, and I wasn't gonna whisper it either. My fashion was part of the message - freedom in every form."

One of your most significant moments was the release of *Purple Rain*, both the album and the film. *It is* a story close to your own.

"It exploded. Caught fire in people's souls. Music, story, pain, beauty - all at once. That was me - The Kid - trying to escape the past, find love, and stay true to the music. It didn't coddle anyone. It was raw - family trauma, artistic rivalry, and redemption.

People weren't used to a pop star being that exposed. That's why it landed. Purple Rain wasn't about fame, but becoming who you are when the world pulls at every piece of you.

That album sold over 25 million copies. That changed things. That's when the world saw me. I wasn't just the weird kid from Minneapolis anymore - I was global.

But success brings chains. People wanted to package me, control me, and claim me. I had to fight to own my masters, name, and voice.

They called me difficult. I called it freedom. I wasn't fighting for fame - I was fighting to own my name, my songs, my soul. Most artists don't even know they're in a war until it's too late. I wanted to win mine so they wouldn't have to start theirs from zero."

You inspired others. Do you consider yourself a Muse?

Prince grins. "That's a word with edges. I don't sit in a corner, whispering ideas. I ignite. You don't come to me for a nudge - you catch fire or don't.

People watched what I did - how I moved, played, and lived - and sometimes that stirred something in them. If that lights someone else up? Beautiful.

But I never set out to be a Muse. I set out to be real. And sometimes, real is more inspiring than perfect."

Do you ever feel like the music is coming through you rather than from you?

"All the time. I don't even remember writing some of the best stuff I've ever made. It's like the universe borrowed me for a minute.

I'd be in the studio for 12 hours, without food or sleep, and come out with a whole album. That's not hustle - that's channelling.

Songs like When Doves Cry, or Sometimes It Snows in April - those weren't planned. They arrived. That's the difference between a hit and a hymn. One entertains. The other... lifts."

Some of your songs face pain and injustice head-on. Do you see yourself as an activist?

"I never carried a sign. But I carried the truth. Sign o' the Times was protest, wrapped in a groove. If I can make you dance and think - then I'm doing something right."

What's one truth you tried to tell, even when people didn't want to hear it?

"That being different is divine. That love isn't neat. That vulnerability isn't weakness.

That when a Black boy breaks, it doesn't mean he's broken forever. That we survive and shine - not despite the scars, but because of them."

You created Paisley Park for more than yourself. Was it always meant to be a space for others, too?

"Yeah. It was a haven. A place where you can dream loud. I sometimes open it to the public, hold concerts and surprise shows, and let people feel the current. Art needs a temple. This is mine."

What do you hope young Black artists take from your path?

"That you don't have to ask permission to be powerful. Own your masters. Own your vision. And never, ever shrink to fit someone else's frame."

You influenced Sheila E. and Wendy & Lisa.

"They were already lightning. I just made sure they struck. Sheila had rhythm running through her bones, and Wendy & Lisa? They heard in colour.

I didn't teach them anything - they showed me how to stretch. What I did was give them space and let them fly. That's the job. Not control. Collaboration. When they soared, the whole world lifted a little."

Stevie Nicks said *Little Red Corvette* inspired her song *Stand Back*.

"She called me and played it over the phone. Said, '*You sparked this.*' That meant something. Music is like a chain reaction - one note can set off a whole fire.

I dropped by and laid down the synth parts on the spot. Didn't ask for anything. Didn't need credit. That track wasn't mine to own.

If the music calls me, I show up, serve the moment, then disappear back into the ether."

You had a real creative fire with Sheila E.

"Sheila had stardust in her veins. I wrote The Glamorous Life for her. That wasn't just a track - it was her stepping out in gold."

And Wendy & Lisa?

"Alchemists. I'd toss out a chord, and they'd paint galaxies. Sometimes, It Snows in April. That was us feeling grief, raw and unfiltered. They weren't just backing musicians. They were architects."

You also worked with Vanity and Apollonia.

Prince chuckles. "Vanity burned bright - she lit up a room and made no apologies. I wanted bold, wild women who owned the stage, not just stood on it.

Apollonia brought something different: sultry, sharp, in control. 'Sex Shooter' and 'Nasty Girl' weren't background - they were declarations. Those women weren't just part of the show. They were the fire."

You didn't just influence. You shared.

"Of course. Why dim someone else's light? My light gets stronger when others blaze too."

Prince glides toward a purple guitar resting in a shaft of skylight. He plucks a single note - bright, bent, echoing - and lets it hang in the air like a question no one dares answer.

You even inspired D'Angelo. He called you a Muse.

"That brother's got depth. Didn't need me to tell him anything. He just knew. We met once or twice, real brief, but the connection was there. It wasn't about words - it was about vibration.

Sometimes, you don't need a conversation to pass the torch. You just need presence. D'Angelo felt that. I saw it in his eyes, heard it in his phrasing."

Many artists call you a role model. What would you say to young creatives now?

"Don't let 'em box you in. If they call you weird, say thank you. Protect your art like it's your breath. That's your truth."

You once said music is a kind of prayer. Is that still true for you?

"Absolutely. Music is devotion - an offering. Sometimes, I'm just the vessel. The melody comes, the words follow, and I don't even know what it means until later. That's spirit talking. That's God in the groove."

You've changed names, personas, and styles. Was reinvention a shield - or a liberation?

"Both. Sometimes, it was armour. Other times, it was wings. Becoming 'The Artist' - that wasn't a stunt. That was me refusing to be property.

I wasn't gonna let a label define me. I had to remind folks: the name's not the power. The work is."

You've written extensively about eternity, rebirth, and leaving the physical. What do you think happens after we die?

"I think we keep playing, just in another frequency. Energy doesn't end - it moves. We turn to light. Or music. Or both."

He sets down the guitar, eyes lit like distant stars. The room stills for a moment, as if the air is holding its breath. He looks up:

"Music heals. As long as there's hurt in the world and funk in the ether? I'm not done. Not even close."

THE MUSE PERSPECTIVE

Prince was never a mirror. He was a prism. The light passed through him and emerged transformed - bolder, stranger, truer.

He didn't follow inspiration; he was it so others could follow."

He shattered templates and rebuilt them in purple. Janelle Monáe, Lizzo, and even Beyoncé testify to his enduring power in sound, spirit, and freedom.

To be moved by Prince was to feel suddenly possible.

He sold over 100 million records, broke gender binaries, and stretched his voice from falsetto fire to baritone balm. He played over 20 instruments, built Paisley Park, and left vaults of unreleased brilliance. Even death couldn't finish his sentence.

Prince died at Paisley Park, aged fifty-seven, in the place he built to house the future.

He left behind a vast array of unreleased material in a custom-built bank vault under his home, including fully completed albums and over 50 finished videos.

But the echo remains. And the spark? Still catching.

NOTE: An Icon's Odyssey Through Art and Life, Inkline Publishing, 2024, is a succinct compilation of Prince's life, not an elaborate biographical study.

For a genuine insider's view of the artist and his impact on others, you may enjoy the visually rich book Prince: A Portrait of the Artist in Memories and Memorabilia by Paul Sexton, published by Welbeck in 2021.

NOTE 1: WHY IT MAKES PERFECT SENSE TO TALK TO DEAD PEOPLE

Conversing with deceased historical figures is not quite as bizarre as it sounds.

For example, when developing his theories, Albert Einstein visualised conversations with past science talents such as Isaac Newton and James Clerk Maxwell, the Scottish physicist and mathematician responsible for the classical theory of electromagnetic radiation.

Imaginary dialogues allowed Einstein to test his ideas against the wisdom of other geniuses, pushing beyond traditional boundaries of thought.

Likewise, the 16th-century French philosopher Michel de Montaigne often engaged in imaginary conversations with Socrates, Seneca, and Plutarch.

He claimed these interchanges allowed one to "rub and polish our brain by contact with others. Closer to our own time, Professor Brett Kahr resurrected from the dead Donald Winnicott, the English paediatrician and psychoanalyst and invited him for a memorable cup of tea at 87 Chester Square, his former London residence, where the two men discuss Winnicott's life and work in compelling detail.

But why bother to have imaginary conversations with long-dead or even fictional people?

One of the first gains, based on the imaginary experiences of travellers in previous times, is intellectual growth. For example, engaging with great thinkers' thoughts can spark logical curiosity.

Engaging with great past communicators can help enhance your art of persuasion and rhetoric. Their ability to convey powerful messages through words can be an invaluable presentation experience.

Reflecting on how such people express ideas can sharpen your communication skills. Marie Stopes, who launched the first birth control clinics, relentlessly presented her ideas through tireless lecturing, issuing books, pamphlets, and other ways to engage with people. She would have lots to tell you about how she made such an impact!

Imagined dialogues with past figures can help you better understand historical events and their contexts.

"Conversing" with someone like Winston Churchill can provide insight into leadership during times of crisis. His famous quote, "*Success is not final, failure is not fatal: It is the courage to continue that counts*", can help focus on the importance of resilience in adversity.

Understanding history through these conversations may enable you to appreciate the complexities of the past and inform your perspective on current events.

Imaginary discussions can be a mirror for self-exploration. Engaging with someone like Virginia Woolf can prompt reflections on one's identity.

Woolf's belief that "for most of history, Anonymous was a woman" can lead one to think critically about one's place and how experiences shape one's identity.

Finally, engaging with the greats can spark creativity. Talking with now-inaccessible artists like Picasso, writers like James Joyce, or musicians like Beethoven can inspire one's artistic side.

Conversations with the greats can feel wishful or even ludicrous. But they provide a treasure trove of advantages beyond entertainment alone. They engage intellectual curiosity, build emotional literacy and can prompt ethical considerations.

Whether you want inspiration, a cultural perspective or creative bursts, this creative interaction can change how you see life. To paraphrase Franklin D. Roosevelt, "Learn from the past to build your future!

(A slightly longer version of this note also appears in my earlier book, Conversations with Remarkable Women, Red Roof Publishing, 2025)

NOTE 2: DISCLAIMER

This book is a work of fiction and creative exploration. While inspired by extensive research into biographical, mythological, philosophical, and artistic traditions, the dialogues, events, and characters are purely the product of the author's imagination. At no time does the author claim to have met the twenty Muses in real life.

While drawing on factual sources, the author does not claim nor intend to imply any formal real-life correspondence or factual accuracy regarding the historical figures or events.

The content is presented for entertainment and intellectual reflection only. It is not intended as a factual account, scholarly treatise, or a source of historical or biographical truth.

Readers should understand that this work represents a personal and fictional interpretation of abstract ideas, myths, and concepts.

The author expressly disclaims any liability for interpretations, uses, or misuses of the material presented in this book.

NOTE 3: ACKNOWLEDGEMENTS

The unsung stars of many books are the subeditors, who catch mistakes and offer discreet suggestions for improvement. That is especially true of Marvellous Muses.

I fully acknowledge the editorial contribution of my wife, Gillilan, whose meticulous attention to detail left me trailing in the dust. So thank you, Gillian, for being with me on Marvellous Muses. It would be a worse book without your invaluable involvement.

Thanks also to Tessa Blanshard-Phibbs, a talented and utterly reliable designer who created and oversaw the book through to production. Thanks for your patience and coping with my endless and often irrelevant e-mails!

I want to thank Zayn Romano, David Basley, Danny Brown, and the team at Penguin Publishers in the US, who have worked on supporting my books.

NOTE 4: COPYRIGHT

NOTE 5: ANDREW'S PREVIOUS BOOKS

Happiness at Work:
It provides wisdom,
advice, and pract…

★★★★★ 1

Leading the Way:
The Seven Skills to
Engage, Inspire a…

★★★★⯪ 24

Charisma: The
Secrets Of Making
A Lasting Impres…

★★★⯪☆ 10

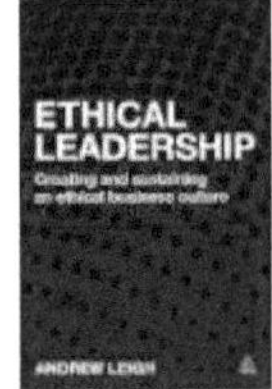

Ethical Leadership:
Creating and
Sustaining an Eth…

★★★★⯪ 9

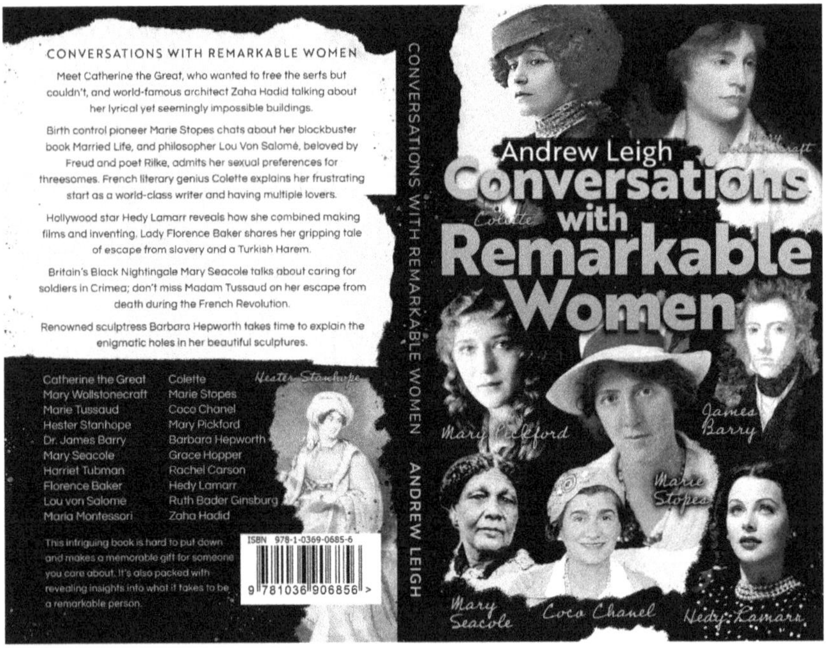

CONVERSATIONS WITH REMARKABLE WOMEN

Meet Catherine the Great, who wanted to free the serfs but couldn't, and world-famous architect Zaha Hadid talking about her lyrical yet seemingly impossible buildings.

Birth control pioneer Marie Stopes chats about her blockbuster book Married Life, and philosopher Lou Von Salomé, beloved by Freud and poet Rilke, admits her sexual preferences for threesomes. French literary genius Colette explains her frustrating start as a world-class writer and having multiple lovers.

Hollywood star Hedy Lamarr reveals how she combined making films and inventing. Lady Florence Baker shares her gripping tale of escape from slavery and a Turkish Harem.

Britain's Black Nightingale Mary Seacole talks about caring for soldiers in Crimea; don't miss Madam Tussaud on her escape from death during the French Revolution.

Renowned sculptress Barbara Hepworth takes time to explain the enigmatic holes in her beautiful sculptures.

Catherine the Great
Mary Wollstonecraft
Marie Tussaud
Hester Stanhope
Dr. James Barry
Mary Seacole
Harriet Tubman
Florence Baker
Lou von Salomé
Maria Montessori

Colette
Marie Stopes
Coco Chanel
Mary Pickford
Barbara Hepworth
Grace Hopper
Rachel Carson
Hedy Lamarr
Ruth Bader Ginsburg
Zaha Hadid

This intriguing book is hard to put down and makes a memorable gift for someone you care about. It's also packed with revealing insights into what it takes to be a remarkable person.

ISBN 978-1-0369-0685-6

Andrew Leigh
Conversations with Remarkable Women

Red Roof Publications
Red Roof, Church Path,
London SW19 3HL

Contact: andrewsbooks@btinternet.com

Website: andrewsbooks.site

eBook ISBN: 979-8-89795-390-5
Paperback ISBN: 979-8-89795-391-2
Hardcover ISBN: 979-8-89795-392-9

For every copy of this book sold,
50p will be donated to the charity: